FIERCE

A CURVY GIRL ROMANTIC SUSPENSE

F-BOMB: CURVY VIGILANTES
BOOK 4

MARY E THOMPSON

BluEyed Press

F-BOMB: CURVY VIGILANTES

Say hello to the Curvy Vigilantes, a group of plus-size women who protect their city. They have no training, but they don't need it. All they need is the desire to right wrongs and to protect the ones they love... and maybe some help from the men strong (and smart) enough to fall for these kick-ass curvy women.

F-BOMB: CURVY VIGILANTES

Forsaken (subscriber exclusive)

Fury

Framed

Feign

Fierce

Fatal

Fear

Flee

Fracture

Faith

To every woman who has ever doubted her own strength... you can do anything and you are powerful beyond your imagination. Never give up.

1

MACKENZIE CHAMBERS SHOOK AS SHE HUNG UP THE PHONE. IT was happening again. No. It couldn't. A woman was dead, and her killer was trying to get away with it.

She couldn't believe she answered both calls. After the man called, she immediately dispatched police. When he hung up, the line rang again. What were the odds Mackenzie would be the one to speak to both of them?

She knew she shouldn't have said anything to Jessica German. She should have listened and done her job. But her head spun and her heart broke and she couldn't keep her mouth shut. Not when she knew what the woman was trying to do.

Mackenzie logged off and walked away from her desk. She needed a minute. She jammed two dollars into the machine and selected a pop. It dropped to the bottom, where she grabbed it. She twisted off the top and tipped the bottle to her lips, enjoying the sweet fizziness.

"Hey, Mackenzie. How are you?"

Holden Cross. A paramedic and consummate nice guy. He was always talking to Mackenzie and asking how her day was. They ran into each other almost daily since he worked on the other side of the building. He was cute, if Mackenzie could bring herself to be attracted to him. She usually couldn't bring herself to be open to being attracted to anyone.

"Hey, Holden."

"Whoa, what's wrong?"

Mackenzie shook her head, hating that he could see through her so easily. She couldn't say the words, though. Not when she knew the look she'd get. The look she always got. She loved her job because no one judged her. Not when the only reason they called was because they needed her help. It didn't matter to them that she'd been wrongfully accused of killing her best friend.

But her coworkers were a different story. They knew her story. They knew what she'd been through. And some of them thought she was guilty.

"Rough call?" Holden asked, assessing her with his endless brown eyes. His dark hair was pushed back from his forehead in a stylish way she was surprised hadn't been messed up while he was on duty. He looked put together and perfect, counter to the disaster Mackenzie always was.

Mackenzie nodded and bit her lip.

"I'm sorry, Mack. Is there anything I can do?"

The nickname threw her. Jaclyn was the only person who'd ever called her Mack. Jack and Mack. They were a team. It had been years since she'd heard the nickname. Years since she had anyone in her life she was close to.

Mackenzie shook her head. "I'll be okay. Thanks, Holden."

"You sure?"

Mackenzie forced a smile and made a move to go around him. "I'm sure. Thanks, though."

Holden grabbed her hand and squeezed before she could get past him. His eyes were soft and kind. Understanding. It would be so easy to lean on him for a minute. Just a minute.

Mackenzie pushed away the fantasy of having someone else, anyone, to lean on. She couldn't. She had no idea who she could trust so it was better to not try.

"Thanks, Holden."

He released her, his gaze locked on her as she backed out of the room.

It would be so easy. But she couldn't give in.

EVERY CALL for the next three weeks put Mackenzie on high alert. She was determined to find Jessica German. To make sure she didn't get away with killing her friend. Mackenzie knew she was guilty. Innocent people didn't run.

She got home after another long night with no leads on where the killer was. Mackenzie was getting frustrated. Someone had to be helping Jessica German. It wasn't right.

Mackenzie turned on the news and stopped cold at the reporter's words.

"Jessica German, the woman accused of killing local art therapist, Karli Sloane, was brought into the police station last night. Another man was brought in with her, a man police are now saying was the lead suspect. Ms. German had no connection to the man, and she was released from police custody after being questioned last night. The suspect, Silver James, died before he was police were able to question him. His death is currently under investigation."

There was no way. It was not possible. Mackenzie

watched the report through her tears. She couldn't believe Jessica German was going to get away with it.

Mackenzie hated that a woman died, but even more, that the woman's own friend was to blame. When she got the first call, from the neighbor, her heart stopped. But when the killer called and tried to pretend she was innocent, Mackenzie was furious.

Karli Sloane deserved better than to be forgotten. Better than having her killer go free. Jessica German deserved justice. And Mackenzie was going to make sure she got it.

MACKENZIE SAT in her car outside Braden Wright's house for the third night in a row. She'd watched him and Jessica German come and go for days, smiling and laughing and acting like nothing was wrong. He was living with a woman who was cold and evil. A woman who killed her friend. He could be next.

He was a firefighter, a good man. He saved people. Mackenzie couldn't sit back and let Jessica German kill him. Or anyone else. One thing she knew was people didn't stop with one. Not unless they were caught.

Mackenzie waited until the lights went out behind the drawn curtains, then sighed and accepted she wasn't going to get anything new. She drove home, hating that she hadn't been able to prove Jessica German killed Karli Sloane yet.

Mackenzie was off the next day. With any luck, she would find something. Prove something. If nothing else, she could claim it was a citizen's arrest and force the police to look into the case.

The next day, Mackenzie drove the now familiar roads back to Braden Wright's house. There were more vehicles in the driveway than usual. It looked like he was having a party in the middle of a Friday afternoon. It was the perfect time to tell them all what she knew about Jessica German.

Mackenzie snuck to the door, praying she didn't have to use the pepper spray she kept tucked in her handbag. She wrapped her hand around it just in case. Then she twisted the doorknob gently. It turned. It was unlocked.

Mackenzie didn't stop to think about what she was doing, she just acted. She burst into the house, finding the living room full of people. "Stop! This is a citizen's arrest. Jessica German, you are guilty of killing... you."

Karli Sloane sat on a couch across the room. Mackenzie knew her face, right down to the birthmark on her neck. How was she alive? What was going on?

"Who are you?" Braden Wright demanded, putting himself between Mackenzie and Jessica.

"I'm Mackenzie Chambers. I came to arrest her." Mackenzie pointed at the woman she was there for.

Jessica stood and moved around Braden. "I recognize your voice. You were the nine-one-one operator. You're the one who thought I killed Karli."

"You did. I know you did. But how..." Mackenzie's gaze shifted to Karli Sloane. "You're not dead. How are you not dead?"

"I'm not, but another woman was killed in my apartment that day." Karli's voice was even and solid.

"How is this not public knowledge? The police—"

"Are aware of the situation," another man said, stepping toward Mackenzie. "I'm Captain Marcus Patrick. This is Adam Johnson with the FBI. His partner is Lorelei Sloane, sitting next to her cousin."

The police captain and FBI agent blocked Mackenzie's view of Karli and her cousin. Mackenzie stared back at the men. "Who was the woman who died?" Panic filled her. Something wasn't right. The whole thing wasn't right.

"Her name was Tonya Warren. She came here because her cousin was missing."

"Why was she killed?"

The police captain and FBI agent exchanged a glance. After a second, Captain Patrick stepped forward. "Ms. Chambers, I know your story. I read your personnel file after Jessica's call. I know about your roommate."

There it was. The look Mackenzie hated. The assurance that she'd been the real killer. Her argument got stuck in her throat. "I didn't kill her."

"Marcus," Karli said from behind the men. "May I?"

Karli moved past Captain Patrick and took Mackenzie's hand. Karli led Mackenzie to a seat and sat next to her.

Mackenzie swallowed her fear and emotions, both sticking in her throat as she looked at the woman she'd believed was dead.

Karli smiled kindly at her, then spoke. "I was in my apartment when Tonya broke in. I was scared, so I left through the fire escape. I didn't have my phone or ID, so when Jessica found her, and my personal items were there, the assumption was she was me. We look enough alike that it was reasonable, even I saw it when I saw her. I didn't believe it was an accident, which left me to think they thought she was me, and someone wanted me dead. The man who had her killed is Damon Street."

"Who?" Mackenzie asked.

"We believe he runs a criminal organization in the area. He moves guns, people, drugs, anything he can through legal organizations that may or may not know what he's doing," the FBI agent explained.

"Why would he care about you?" Mackenzie asked Karli.

"He didn't. He was after my roommate. She dated him without knowing who he was. She left when he almost killed her one night. He wants her back because he believes she belongs to him."

"What? No. She doesn't deserve that." No person belonged to another. No one had a claim over another.

"Thank you," a brown-haired woman Mackenzie hadn't noticed before said. "Damon is evil. I didn't realize it until it was almost too late for me. But I'd gladly sacrifice myself if it means no one else is hurt."

"You can't do that. A man like that will never stop hurting people. I can't tell you how many calls I get every day like that. Many times it's the same woman over and over again, but they always go back. Until they can't." Mackenzie couldn't bear to think of the woman across from her going back to a man who would surely kill her. Not when he was clearly not afraid to kill people.

The woman hugged herself, running her hands up and down her arms. Karli reached out to her, taking her friend's hand.

"Damon thought I was dead," Karli explained to Mackenzie. "When he thought that, Raina was safer. But he knows I'm alive. And he's on the run. He also knows where Tonya's cousin is. She's alive, and we believe he can tell us where. Marcus, Adam, and Lorelei are planning a press conference for this afternoon. That's why we're all here. We're discussing what we're going to say and how we're going to get the public's help to bring Damon in."

"I promise you, I will make sure he pays. I will do whatever I can to help. I hear things. I might be able to help find Tonya's cousin. The calls I take... Let me help. Please." Mackenzie looked around the room at the group gathered there. She wasn't sure she was wrong about the situation, but if she was, she was not going to let a man like that go free.

"We're asking everyone to help," the FBI agent said. "But not all of what we're going to tell you is public information. If you're willing—"

"I'm willing. Tell me what I can do. I won't stop until he's brought to justice. I promise you." Mackenzie met Karli's gaze and nodded.

"Good. Then let's get started," the FBI agent said.

Mackenzie listened as they detailed what they knew so far. Damon Street was a sick man who preyed on innocent people. Mackenzie wondered how many calls she'd taken from people who were victims of his.

As they laid out their plans for the press conference, she kept her gaze on Jessica German. The woman looked ordinary. Her expressions fit what was expected when talking about a man like Damon Street, but Mackenzie wasn't convinced Jessica German was innocent. A woman was still dead, and just because it wasn't the woman they all thought, didn't mean Jessica German had nothing to do with it.

"Are you going to be able to keep all of this to yourself?" Captain Patrick asked Mackenzie.

She nodded and smiled at him. She'd never met the man before, but she knew of him. He seemed to be a man of integrity and honor. It was the only reason Mackenzie was willing to put a pin in her suspicions and let things play out.

"How is it no one knows who this man is?" Mackenzie asked. It was the question she was most curious about. If Damon Street was so bad, how had he evaded police custody for so long?

"Damon is smart," an older woman said. "He's been working the city for decades. He knows everything there is to know about how things operate here. We believe he has a network that extends into the police department, which has allowed him to stay undetected."

"Into the police department?" Mackenzie asked.

Captain Patrick nodded. "Unfortunately, yes. We're not sure who his contact, or contacts, is, but it's unlikely he doesn't have at least one. We think that's how Silver James was killed. He was given water that had been poisoned. The officer who gave it to him has been cleared of all wrongdoing, but someone put drugs in the bottle. Someone who knew it would end up in the hands of the man who could tell us everything about Damon Street."

"Wow," Mackenzie breathed. If she didn't have trust issues before, she definitely had them after that. The police couldn't even be trusted? How would she know who to go to? What if she heard something?

"Are we all clear on the plan for today?" the FBI agent asked. He looked beyond Mackenzie to Raina, still standing in the doorway.

Raina nodded, as did everyone else.

"What plan are you talking about?" Mackenzie asked.

The others exchanged a glance. They weren't sure if they wanted to tell her the rest. She knew about the press conference, but there was more. More that she didn't know about.

"Never mind. I get it. None of you know me, and you have no way of knowing if I'm involved in this somehow. If I find out something I think could help, who should I be in touch with?" Mackenzie asked, moving on before they could make excuses for why they didn't want her to know everything.

"Me," Captain Patrick said. He stepped forward and pulled out his phone. "Put your number in here so I know it's you. I'll give you mine, too. I always have my phone with me. You can call me anytime, day or night. Please don't call anyone else on the police force. Not until we know who we can trust."

"I won't trust any of them," Mackenzie said, knowing none of them understood how true that statement was.

"We need to go," another man said, holding hands with a woman who'd been more comforting to Raina than talkative the entire time. "We have to get the boys from school."

The woman hugged the others while the man nodded to everyone.

"Thanks for your help, Wray and Stacey," Captain Patrick said. "And thanks for bringing lunch."

"The least we could do. We'll see everyone soon," Stacey said.

The others moved around, but they all seemed to be staying put. Waiting. Mackenzie realized they were waiting for her to leave.

"I guess I should go, too. Is it okay if I come to the press conference?" she asked.

Captain Patrick nodded. "Absolutely. We appreciate your help. And I'm truly sorry about Jaclyn. And everything you went through. I know it doesn't make up for it, but I've heard good things about the work you do and know it's very important. You're exceptionally kind, Mackenzie. Thank you for working with us."

Mackenzie was oddly touched by his statement. Maybe he was placating her, or maybe he was keeping her close so he could watch her, or maybe he was sincere, but his words made her trust him just a little.

Maybe Jessica German was innocent and Mackenzie had been wrong. Or maybe she was the mastermind behind Damon Street. An abusive man who'd been operating for that long didn't do it alone. He had a team. And if he was that fragile with his emotions, he usually had a boss. One who was smarter and stronger and more dangerous than him.

Was Damon the one in charge? Or did he have a boss he got his orders from? Could Jessica German be that boss?

Mackenzie was going to find out. And make sure justice was served.

2

———

Holden sipped his coffee and watched the press conference. If the police captain wasn't the one delivering the news, Holden wouldn't have believed the story. It was definitely a doozy.

"So, who's the dead woman?" Holden's partner and friend, Spencer, asked. Holden and Spencer had been paired together for over a year, but they'd worked the same shift off and on much longer. Spencer was a little taller than Holden, with light brown skin and eyes that were the most unique golden-brown Holden had ever seen. Spencer joked his eyes were magical because when patients looked into them, they immediately calmed down. Holden thought Spencer was full of it until he saw it happen.

"Sounds like someone random. Wrong place, wrong time."

"That's some shit luck."

Holden nodded. Spencer was not wrong. What were the odds a woman who could have been Karli Sloane's twin ended up in her apartment the same time someone broke in to kill her? Not good, if Holden had to guess.

"Do they really think they're going to find this Damon Street guy?"

Holden shook his head. "If he's as much of a ghost as he seems, I can't imagine how, but Captain Patrick is pretty good. The only reason I would think he'd be talking about this is if he thinks the public can help."

Spencer snorted. "The public is usually more oblivious than stupid. Our last guest being the perfect example."

Holden couldn't help but laugh. The man they took to the hospital had been walking to work, texting a friend and not paying attention to where he was going. He stepped out into traffic, narrowly avoiding getting hit, but when someone blew their horn, he dropped his phone. The guy bent down to pick up the phone and knocked himself out when he whacked his head on a sideview mirror. The driver of the car called it in.

The guy was awake by the time Holden and Spencer got there, insisting he was fine and didn't need to go to the hospital. He walked off and ran right into a street sign. He didn't argue after that and let them drop him off at St. Nicholas Hospital.

"That dude would have walked off the bridge and into the Falls if he'd been going that way. I swear, there isn't anything on my phone that's ever that interesting where I won't look up and see where I'm going."

"What if Leah is texting you?" Holden asked. Leah and Spencer were high school sweethearts and were married right after college. They had three kids and the kind of life Holden hoped to have one day. If he could catch Mackenzie's eye.

"Leah knows if it's important to call me. Nothing that major comes through on a text."

Holden nodded in agreement. Their patient would have been a lot better off if he'd looked up from the phone.

Spencer's radio squawked with an incoming call. "Need assistance at two-four-seven Pineview Drive. Man in distress. Possible heart attack."

"Show us responding. On our way," Spencer said.

Holden was already climbing into the passenger side of the ambulance when Spencer cranked up the vehicle and pulled out. Once they were clear of the bay doors, he hit the siren and took off.

"No Mackenzie today?" Spencer asked as he drove the city streets without hesitation.

Holden shook his head. His partner knew about his interest in Mackenzie. Holden thought the only one who didn't know was likely Mackenzie herself. Or maybe that was just what he told himself so he could hold on to hope that she might be interested in him one day.

"She's off today."

"Didn't she take the calls for that case on the news? About the dead woman who was killed by the friend?"

Holden nodded. He remembered how shaken up Mackenzie looked that day. He didn't know what the cause was at the time, but once the story came out, Holden knew it got to her. And why. Mackenzie would never hurt another person, but being accused of killing her friend put a mark on her that would never be erased.

"How's she doing with this news?" Spencer asked.

"I don't know."

"You haven't called her?"

"We're not friends like that."

Spencer gave Holden a look that called bullshit.

"Fine, she doesn't see us like that. Whenever I try to talk to her, she gets away from me as quickly as possible."

Spencer pulled over in front of the house they were reporting to and cut the engine. Before he got out, he put a hand on Holden's arm and looked him dead in the eye. Those magical golden eyes caught Holden's attention.

"Don't give up on her, man. She'll see how great you are and realize what she's missing. If you care about her like I know you do, don't give up just yet."

Holden nodded, feeling a confidence he wasn't sure he deserved to feel. Spencer let go of him and grabbed the bag that sat between the seats, and they headed into the house.

THE REST of their shift was endless, one call after another. Holden barely had time to grab something to eat, let alone think about Mackenzie. Although he did think about her, constantly, but he couldn't focus on her.

When their shift ended early in the morning, Holden walked through the shared break room, hoping to catch Mackenzie. He smiled when he saw her getting a cup of coffee. Three creams, three sugars.

"Hey, Mackenzie."

"Hi, Holden." She gave him a tight smile. She had circles under her eyes, and her clothes were wrinkled.

"How was your time off?"

She shrugged and stirred her coffee.

"Did you see the press conference yesterday?"

Her gaze snapped to his. Her eyes narrowed just slightly. "I did." Her words were clipped and tense.

"Crazy story, don't you think?"

"Things are not always what they seem," she said through gritted teeth.

"Yeah, I know. Just seems hard to imagine they don't

have more information about what happened or who the woman is that died."

"Maybe they can't share that information yet."

Holden looked closely at Mackenzie. She was avoiding his gaze and moving toward the door. "Yeah, maybe. Did you see the reports about that big storm we're supposed to get next weekend?" The weather was a safe topic. Maybe he could keep her talking for a few more minutes.

She nodded and reached the door. "Yeah, but I'm sure it won't be as big of a deal as they say. They always want to scare people. We get tons of snow around here all the time."

"True. I hope it's not a big deal. I'm supposed to work when it's scheduled to hit."

"Me too."

Holden couldn't help but smile at that news. Maybe getting stuck at work wouldn't be so bad if he was stuck with Mackenzie.

"I need to get back out there. Have a good day."

"You, too, Mackenzie." He waved as she retreated. Once she turned the corner and was gone, he dropped his hand and shook his head. "Smooth, Cross, real smooth."

Holden crashed hard when he got home. He hadn't gotten any rest overnight and was exhausted. It was dark when he woke up again, feeling worse than when he went to bed, if that were possible. Holden fixed himself breakfast, even though it was dinnertime for normal people. He sat on his couch with his food and turned on the TV to drown out the silence of his apartment.

The news replayed parts of the press conference again, then went on to talk about the local sports teams, other events happening around town, and the upcoming storm they were projecting.

"It's still a long way out, but this storm could overwhelm

the city. We're staying in close contact with city officials to make sure they're as prepared as possible. For anyone with travel plans, you might want to start thinking about alternative options," the weatherman said.

Holden watched the report and shook his head. Like Mackenzie said, they were used to snow. The city was prepared. There was no way it would be as bad as they were predicting.

MACKENZIE HUNG up the phone and sighed. She could almost smile after that one. A woman called after she was rear-ended on her way home from work. She was shaken up, but mostly okay. Crappy start to the woman's week. Mackenzie spoke to her until the paramedics and police arrived. They were taking her to the hospital for evaluation, but the paramedic said the woman should be fine.

The thanks of the woman was what kept Mackenzie going through long shifts and bad calls. Not all calls were easy. Most weren't. But the ones that ended with good news were the ones that made it all worthwhile.

The phone rang again, and Mackenzie tapped to receive the call.

"Nine-one-one, what is your emergency?"

"Help... me," the voice on the other end whispered.

"Can you tell me where you are?" Mackenzie's pulse jumped at the ragged breath the caller took.

"Can't see. I'm in... ditch."

"You're in a ditch?" Mackenzie waved over her supervisor and handed Amanda a headset so she could hear the woman on the phone.

"I was pushed from a car."

"Do you know where you could be? Do you know where you were when you were pushed? Is there anything visible? Any buildings or street signs? Anything so we can find you?"

The woman coughed. For several long seconds, Mackenzie listened as the woman gagged and coughed. She spit. "Blood. He beat me. Oh, God, that's not good."

"Who beat you?" Mackenzie blurted.

"Damon Street. He was supposed to take me somewhere safe, but he lied. He said I was revenge." She wheezed, struggling to get the words out.

Damon Street. Mackenzie struggled to breathe. He'd hurt someone else. Mackenzie had been hoping to hear something about him for three days, since she first heard the name, but now that she had, she wished she could go back. "Can you tell me your name?"

"Penny."

"Okay, Penny. We're going to find you. How many lanes wide is the road?" Mackenzie needed someone to find this woman. She was a key to Damon. She could help them bring him down.

"Don't... know," the woman whispered, gasping for breath once more.

"We need more," Amanda whispered. The woman couldn't hear her, but she always whispered to avoid distracting the agents from the call.

"Stay with me, Penny. Where did Damon pick you up?"

"First Street."

"And how far did you drive? How long were you in the car?"

"He took me to a warehouse. I fell asleep. He gave me drugs." Penny started to cry. "I'm sorry. They gave me so many drugs, and it hurts so bad when they take them away. Damon..." Penny was silent was a long moment.

Amanda walked away just far enough to make a call without Mackenzie hearing and getting distracted. Likely to the carrier to get a trace on Penny's phone.

"Penny! Are you still there?" Mackenzie shouted, fear spiking through her. Penny was dying. Whether from the drugs, Damon, or the cold, she was dying. They had to find her fast. Her gaze snapped to Amanda and held as she waited for Penny to reply.

Penny sucked in a breath and groaned. "Hurts so much. Broken." She wheezed. "I'm tired. I might take a nap."

"Penny! No. Wake up, Penny. I need you to tell me where you are."

"I... hear... traffic. Truck. Water." She coughed again. "So cold."

"We're going to find you, Penny." Tears streamed down Mackenzie's cheeks. Listening to someone struggling to hold on was the worst part of her job. Best-case scenario, a good samaritan or paramedic would get there and save her. Mackenzie didn't always get best-case scenario.

"The carrier gave us an approximate location. The phone isn't hers, but they gave it to us anyway," Amanda whispered.

"Whose phone is it?"

"Damon's," Penny said. "Stole from him."

"Smart, Penny. You're smart."

She coughed a laugh. "No one agrees. If true, I wouldn't be here."

"We're on the way, Penny. Just hang on a little longer."

"Don't leave me," she whispered. Penny sniffed, her voice fading.

"I'm right here, Penny. I'm not going anywhere."

"Keep her talking," Amanda said.

"Where are you from, Penny? Did you grow up in

Western New York?" Mackenzie wiped her tears and cleared her throat. She had a job to do. It was up to her to keep Penny alive until the paramedics found her. She said a silent prayer Holden was out there. Mackenzie didn't trust herself with Holden, but she knew he was good. He wouldn't give up until he brought Penny to safety.

"No," Penny choked. "Texas. Love snow."

"We have plenty of that," Mackenzie said, struggling to keep her voice light. "We're supposed to get more snow over the weekend. What's your favorite thing to do in the snow? I enjoy sledding."

Penny laughed softly. Her breathing was shallow and slow. "Cold."

"Sledding is cold. Do you like to sit inside and watch it snow? That's how my best friend was." Mentioning Jaclyn sent a spear through Mackenzie, but it reminded her Penny was counting on her. She wasn't giving up.

"Fire... nice. Now."

"They'll get you warmed up soon, Penny."

She wheezed, then choked.

"Penny, are you okay?"

Penny continued to choke. She coughed, then wheezed again, a deep breath that led to silence.

"Penny?"

Mackenzie looked up at Amanda. They both held their breath.

"Penny? Are you still there?"

Silence answered her. A vehicle drove by, then another. It was quiet wherever Penny was. Damon was smart.

"Maybe she dropped the phone. She could have passed out. Penny!" Amanda shouted into Mackenzie's headset.

A siren sounded through the phone, and Amanda lifted

her other phone, stepping away. "She's close to you. We hear the siren through the phone she was using."

Mackenzie stared at her screen, waiting for someone to tell her what was going on.

The siren gave way to the loud crunch of tires on the snow-covered side of the road, then voices. Amanda continued to give directions as the voices grew louder until one of them shouted, "Found her!"

"Oh, thank God," Amanda whispered. "Is she alive?"

The phone Penny was using crackled before someone spoke. "We have her. She's not breathing. She's blue head-to-toe. Someone didn't want her to survive. She's barely dressed."

"Jesus," Amanda whispered.

"Thank you. If you could, please let us know. This is Mackenzie."

"Hey, Mackenzie. This is Donahue. We'll do our best."

"Thank you."

Mackenzie hung up the phone and looked up at Amanda.

"That was a tough one, I know," Amanda said. "Why don't you take a minute?"

Mackenzie nodded and started to get up when the phone rang again. Without thinking twice, Mackenzie answered the call.

"Nine-one-one. What is your emergency?"

"Take a break," Amanda whispered, putting her hand on Mackenzie's shoulder before she walked away.

Mackenzie nodded, then focused on the caller. She couldn't do anything else for Penny. But she could help the person currently on the line.

MACKENZIE WAS ALMOST DONE with her shift when her phone rang. It was an internal call, not a public one. Mackenzie hoped it was news about Penny. "This is Mackenzie."

"Hey, Mackenzie, this is Donahue."

"Hey. Thanks for calling me. How's Penny?"

"We lost her, unfortunately."

"Oh, no."

"Yeah. We did everything we could, Mackenzie. She was already gone when we got there, but Amanda said it wasn't long so we were hoping she would come back, but she didn't. No pulse, no heartbeat on the way to the hospital. They tried to warm her up and get her back, but once her core temp was back up, they still couldn't get her body to come back. I wanted to call you."

Mackenzie drew in a slow breath and closed her eyes. "Thank you for letting me know."

"Yeah. I'm sorry, Mackenzie. We really did try."

Makenzie smiled. "I know you did, Donahue. Thank you." She reached to hang up, then remembered the cell phone. "Donahue!"

"Yeah?"

"The phone Penny was using. What happened to it?"

"Not sure. We handed it over to the hospital with her. Why?"

"Because it wasn't hers. It belonged to the man who hurt her."

"The hospital should have it. They have protocols and all that. I'm sure the state she was in would prompt an investigation."

"Yeah, I'm sure. Thanks again, Donahue." Mackenzie pulled out her personal phone and was scrolling for Captain Patrick's number as she hung up from Donahue's call. She logged out of her computer, listening to the phone ring on the other end.

"Patrick."

"A woman died today. She had a cell phone on her. It was his."

"Excuse me?" Captain Patrick said. A door closed on his end of the line. "Are you saying what I think you're saying?"

"I got a call earlier. Her name was Penny. I listened while she died. She said he told her he was going to save her and tricked her and she was revenge. He beat her and dumped her body on the side of a road. She stole his phone and called me from it."

"How did she get your number?"

"She didn't call me directly. But I was the one who answered when she called nine-one-one."

"You really are in the right place at the right time."

"I couldn't save her," Mackenzie whispered, the emotions of the call sinking in and spilling out.

"You did your best."

"It wasn't enough. He's going to keep hurting people, keep killing people. You need to get that phone."

"I'm on it. Thank you for the call. I appreciate your help on this."

"No one else is going to die if I have a say in it."

"Same."

3

___

Damon Street watched the news with a smirk. Any second there would be a report about Trevor's whore being dead. There was little doubt in Damon's mind Trevor knew she was missing, but once he found out the bitch was dead, he'd come for Damon.

Damon was going to be ready for him.

He sipped his beer and listened to the bar around him. He paid cash and made sure he was indistinguishable from half the men there. His hat was low over his eyes, and he sat on the end away from others. When the crowd cheered for whatever stupid sporting event they were watching, Damon pretended to be happy. The only thing that was going to make him happy was to resume his position within the Company and send Trevor packing.

"A woman was killed today," the reporter said, piquing Damon's interest. He smiled and straightened in his seat.

"Her body was dumped on the side of the road. The nine-one-one call she made said she was beaten and killed by a man named Damon Street. Police are asking for anyone who knows the whereabouts of the man on your screen to please call the confidential tip line. Viewers will remember Street was also involved in the attempted murder of local art therapist, Karli Sloane. A murder that left Tonya Warren dead instead. Street is considered armed and dangerous and anyone who believes they have spotted him is encouraged not to approach the man but to notify police immediately of his presumed location."

Damon shifted in his seat. How in the fuck did that waste of flesh get a phone? Damon tried to think back. The burner he had was… Where was it? Fuck. Was it possible she snatched it from somewhere?

With a growl, Damon tossed a few bills on the bar and stood. He kept his head down, carefully avoiding bumping into anyone, a challenge when the team on TV scored and the crowd went crazy. A man stepped out in front of Damon and held up his hand for a high-five, not moving until Damon returned the gesture. Thankfully, the man's glassy gaze said he was too drunk to recognize himself in the mirror, let alone a wanted man.

When Damon was outside, he hit the button on the car keys he stole from the drunk guy. He was doing the public a service not letting that man drive home. Damon got into the car and pulled out slowly, like he was the owner of the vehicle and nothing out of the ordinary was happening.

The motel Damon was staying at let him pay cash and didn't ask any questions. He ditched the vehicle half a mile away, pointing it in the opposite direction, and walked. After checking that the tape he left on the door was in place and nothing in his room had moved, Damon tore the place apart, looking for his phone.

It was gone.

"Fuck!" he yelled in the empty room.

He had to move. If they had his phone, they might be

able to track where he'd been. Damon packed up the clothes he'd been washing and wearing since Mick was killed. He plugged the sink and the tub, then turned the water on in both. The police would show up eventually, and when they did, he needed to make sure they had as little DNA evidence as possible. Damon threw the sheets and towels on the floor and wiped down as many surfaces as possible to remove his fingerprints. The water was just beginning to spill over the edge of the sink when Damon let himself out of the unit.

Damon needed to be smarter about how he worked. He couldn't risk the police catching up to him. Or Trevor. Damon knew he could overpower the little fuckwad, but Trevor had the Company resources. Damon needed to outsmart him if he was going to win.

And Damon was going to win. He was going to distract Trevor enough for him to lower his guard, then he was going to go in for the kill and prove to the boss he had more value than Trevor. And when he was back in power, Raina would pay for her part in Damon's temporary downfall. Once and for all.

HOLDEN WALKED into the weight room just as Donahue said Mackenzie's name.

"Mackenzie got the worst of it. Hearing someone die and not being able to help has to suck," Donahue said. He was older, pushing fifty, and had been on the job for decades. Holden had a lot of respect for the man and the way he handled himself. Donahue never let anyone talk poorly about another person. Everyone was equal for him.

"At least when we're there we can do something. That

woman was never going to make it, though. Not dressed like she was. Damn shame," Ackerman said. He was new to the job and was paired with Donahue so he was trained right. Seemed to be working so far.

"What happened?" Holden asked.

Donahue met his gaze. "Mackenzie got a call from a woman who'd been dumped from a vehicle. She was barely dressed and mostly dead when she was pushed out of the car. Had a stolen phone and couldn't tell Mackenzie where she was, so Amanda had to get the carrier to give us a location. She was dead when we got there. We tried, the hospital tried, but there was nothing any of us could do."

"Shit. How's Mackenzie?"

Donahue shrugged. "You know Mackenzie. She doesn't let anything get to her. She sounded a little off. Hard not to be."

"When was this?"

"Yesterday. End of her shift. We were just getting started."

"Thanks." Holden knew he needed to get his workout in, but more than that, he needed to see for himself that Mackenzie was okay.

Holden raced down the hallway, trying not to run while not delaying at all. He was almost to the break room when someone stepped out from a supply closet right in front of him.

"Hey, handsome," Isabel said with a seductive grin. "Where are you going in such a hurry? Looking for me?" She slid her hand up his chest and tugged his neck. She took a step back toward the supply closet, gazing at him through her long black lashes with those violet eyes he fell for when they first met.

"No, actually," Holden said. He refused to let her pull

him into the closet. It wouldn't be the first time they'd used that space, but he was done with her. Had been for months. Since she laughed at him when he mentioned wanting to train to be a flight paramedic.

"Are you still mad at me about that flight thing?" She chuckled. "Honey, people who look like you and me don't need extra training. We just need to smile and we get our way."

He removed her hands from around his neck and pushed them back toward her. Isabel had been nothing more than a distraction for Holden. Someone to have some fun with. She made him feel good, and he was weak enough to think that was enough for him at one time. "Maybe that's how you want to go through life, but I intend to help people."

She scoffed and rolled her eyes. "You are helping people. Being a flight paramedic is not better just because it's different."

"I never said it was better. Just that I wanted to try it out. See if I liked it." Holden blew out a breath slowly. He was letting her distract him, and he didn't have time. Mackenzie was likely leaving soon. "I need to go. I don't have time for this."

"What—"

Holden didn't stick around to hear her question. He pushed his way into the break room. Mackenzie wasn't in there, but she was headed that way.

Holden went to the snack machine and pretended he was there for a bag of chips. He stared at the options until the door opened behind him. He turned and found her, head down, walking toward him.

"Hey, Mackenzie. I was hoping I'd run into you," Holden said.

Mackenzie looked up at him. Her gaze was unfocused, like she didn't even realize where she was. She sucked in a breath and took a step back. "Holden. Hi. I didn't know anyone else was in here."

Holden smiled at her. "I heard about your call yesterday. How are you?"

"Someone was talking about me?" she gasped.

Holden shook his head. "No, Donahue was talking about the call. He said it was a really tough one. Mentioned you were the one who spoke to the woman who died. He knows you're strong, but I wanted to check on you."

She laughed mirthlessly. "Strong. I'm not strong. I couldn't save that woman. All I did was sit there and listen to her while she died. She was freezing to death, probably bleeding to death, and I was warm and safe on the other end of the phone."

Holden stepped closer to Mackenzie. "That wasn't your fault, Mack. You are there for so many people when they're scared or alone or hurt. Losing someone is painful, but that doesn't mean it's your fault. The person who hurt her, who left her for dead, that's whose fault it is."

Mackenzie swallowed roughly. She looked up at Holden. She shoved her glasses up the bridge of her nose. Her brown eyes were huge up close, almost like a cartoon character. She looked so vulnerable and scared.

"I'm so sorry she didn't survive," Holden whispered.

Mackenzie nodded, not breaking eye contact. "So am I."

Was it his imagination, or did she take a step closer?

"I know Donahue did his best."

Holden nodded. "He did. He always does. He's the best paramedic we have."

Mackenzie shook her head.

"You don't think he is?"

"No. I think you are. If I was ever in trouble, I'd want you to save me."

"Mackenzie."

She lunged at him so fast his head spun. He caught her in his arms, surprise parting his lips when she pressed her lips to his.

Mackenzie's lips were warm and soft, like the rest of her. She was on her tiptoes, her body stretched out against his. Her arms went around his neck. She pulled him closer.

His brain finally kicked in and realized he was kissing Mackenzie Chambers. His hands moved from where they were when he caught her to get in on the action. He slid them across her back, holding her tight to his body as he tilted his head and deepened their kiss.

But as soon as his tongue brushed against hers, she pulled back. Just as quickly as she'd launched herself at him, she was gone. Her hand covered her mouth, blocking him from a second chance. Her other hand pushed on his shoulder.

Holden didn't try to hold on to her. He didn't argue. He didn't say anything. He just stood there as Mackenzie raced out of the break room and away from him as fast as her curvy hips could carry her.

"Dammit."

MACKENZIE KEPT her hand on her mouth until she made it to her desk. She grabbed her headset without thinking and logged back in to take another call. She had ten minutes left on her shift and she could easily walk away, but she needed the distraction.

She hated herself for hoping someone would call, but she hoped someone would call.

Her mind raced as she stared at the phone. She kissed Holden Cross. What was she thinking? He was a good guy, but she was not cut out for a relationship. Especially not with the best looking guy in the building. Holden was nice to her, but he was just nice. He never meant anything by it, and him kissing her back... Well, that had to be his body reacting to a woman. He didn't mean anything by it.

Mackenzie chewed on her nail and tried to calm her breathing. It was sad one kiss made her heart race the way it did, but it had been years since Mackenzie had kissed another person. Since she felt another person's arms around her.

When Jaclyn died, Mackenzie lost a piece of herself. The boyfriend she had at the time stopped calling when she was arrested, and he never called again, even after she was released. Mackenzie wouldn't have wanted him to call, anyway. She was too raw. Trusting another person was out of the question.

It didn't matter that it had been nine years, Mackenzie hadn't let her guard down since. She hadn't spent the night with a man. She hadn't even gotten naked with one. It was a long time before she could even sleep. Long enough that she nearly had to be committed. The only reason she wasn't was because Suzanne forced Mackenzie to sleep. Suzanne became a friend to Mackenzie when she didn't have anyone else. She was the reason Mackenzie became a nine-one-one operator, and the main reason Mackenzie didn't go to jail. Suzanne took Mackenzie's call the day Jaclyn died and fought for her.

But even Suzanne was gone now, and Mackenzie was alone. She had no one in her life. No one to call and talk to about kissing Holden and what a mistake it was. Because it was definitely a mistake.

"Hey, Mackenzie. A few of us were going to grab a drink. Want to join us? It's been a long few days," Eric asked. He sat at the desk on the other side of Mackenzie's and was nice enough. He was also married and friends with everyone who worked with them.

Mackenzie hesitated. It was tempting. She'd been working there for years and hadn't made friends with any of them. She opened her mouth to answer when Isabel, one of the paramedics, walked over.

"Are you ready?" Isabel asked.

Eric nodded and turned back to Mackenzie. "I invited Mackenzie, too."

Isabel followed his gaze and examined Mackenzie. She rolled her eyes and looked at Eric. "Why?"

"Is! Be nice," Eric hissed. He turned back to Mackenzie and smiled. "Sorry. She's a bitch, but we love her. Are you coming?"

Before Mackenzie could answer, her phone rang. She grabbed hold of the excuse and shook her head. "Maybe next time. Have fun."

"See you in a few days," Eric said. He waved and dragged a glaring Isabel away from his desk.

Mackenzie realized the call was a direct call to her line and answered it was a question in her voice. "Hello?"

"Can you talk?" Captain Patrick asked.

"Yes, sir."

"Good. I just wanted to thank you for the advice you gave me. It was the perfect gift for my wife."

Mackenzie took a second. Was she confused? It sounded like Captain Patrick, but the only thing... Oh! He was speaking in code. "You're welcome. I'm happy I could help."

"You were a big help. Because of you, we booked a stay at a new hotel, one we never would have thought to look."

"Really?" Mackenzie breathed. They found Damon.

"Yep. Unfortunately, we weren't able to catch anyone when we stopped by, but I'm confident we will."

Mackenzie sighed. "Oh." They figured out where Damon was, but he was gone by the time the police arrived, if she was understanding things correctly.

"We were disappointed, too. But we're not giving up on finding the right place."

"Good. I'm happy to hear that."

"We know this isn't over."

"No, it's not. Not by a long shot."

"We're still looking."

"I hope so. Have you decided who can be trusted?"

Captain Patrick breathed a laugh. "I'm starting to think you're on that list."

"I am. But I'm not sure everyone you have on that list should be."

"I know you feel that way, but I assure you, you're wrong about that."

"I hope I am."

"You are. Thanks for the advice, Mackenzie. We'll talk soon."

"Yes, sir."

Mackenzie hung up the phone and drew a breath. She'd hoped things would be closer to over by now, but they weren't even a little.

Mackenzie logged out of the system and gathered her things from her desk. She debated apologizing to Holden but figured it was better to just pretend nothing ever happened and avoid him from now on. Besides, she had work to do.

Donahue was kind enough to tell Mackenzie exactly where they picked Penny up. Mackenzie spent the last few days crafting a cross for Penny. She'd never been reported missing, and she had no family that they'd found. Her body would be buried by the state, but no one would ever visit her grave. No one was around to miss her. So Mackenzie designated herself as family to the victims she couldn't help, the ones no one else called family. The women who were abused and murdered by their significant others. The people abandoned and forgotten. The unclaimed of the world.

She would be one of them one day. A body no one would claim. A body no one would care about. Her mother was gone and her father had a new life with his second wife and step-sons. Mackenzie hoped they would care, but the painful reality was they didn't stand by her when she was wrongfully accused of killing her best friend, so she didn't want them by her after that. She considered herself alone. Except for the other unclaimed people who made up her family.

Mackenzie parked on the side of the road near where Penny died. She got out her cross and hammer and moved to the spot highlighted by her headlights. There was still an impression in the dirt where Penny had lain. Right in the middle of that was where Mackenzie put the cross.

When it was in the ground and stable, Mackenzie took a step back. She said a silent prayer that Penny was at peace and that the people who hurt her are brought to justice. And that Mackenzie would be shown the way to make sure justice was served.

4

"THIS STORM IS A ONCE IN A LIFETIME STORM," THE weatherman said. The blue map behind him showed the entire area covered in snow for days.

Holden looked out the windows where snow was already piling up in the parking lot. It was going to be a long shift, even longer if the weather did what they were predicting.

"Niagara County is expected to get five to six feet of snow by this time tomorrow. The city of Buffalo will be a little more, and the Southtowns will be looking at the highest snowfall totals closer to seven or eight feet by the end of this system."

"This is nuts," Spencer said. "I told Leah to stay inside and not to leave for any reason. She said the snow is already up over the three steps outside."

"It's going to get bad," Holden said. "I have a bad feeling we're going to get stuck on a call."

The alarm rang, calling for the first rig of the night. Holden and Spencer traded a look, then rushed out to try to help whoever needed them.

When they made it back to the station, Holden finally let out a breath. The roads were quickly becoming impassable. They had a hard time making it down the street where the house was. An older man had a heart attack, and they barely made it in time to save him. His wife rode in the ambulance to the hospital, knowing it was the only way she'd be with him until after the storm if she stayed home.

"I hope they get more plows out soon," Spencer said as the door closed to the wind and snow outside. "We won't get out again if things get much worse."

Holden nodded. "I wonder how many calls have come in."

"Let's go see how the others are doing. Make a plan for how to manage things. This can get bad."

Holden agreed. It was easy to get overwhelmed when they were dealing with calls on top of each other. Usually they had three crews on a shift, but when there were storms like this, extra teams were brought in to cover. Holden and Spencer were planning to be on duty for two or three days, but there were enough people there that they should get a break.

"How is it out there?" Donahue asked. He was watching the TV in the kitchen, where the other crews were gathered.

"Nasty," Spencer said for them. "Roads are shit. It won't be long before we can't get out."

"That's what I was afraid of. We saw a stuck car, middle of the damn road. Almost hit it trying to get through," Donahue said.

"This is a fucking mess. How in the hell are we going to get to people when they need us?" Spencer asked.

"Not sure. But we need to figure something out. I haven't been around for snow like this before. I don't think the plows are going to be able to keep up. When the roads are full, we're offline."

"When will we know that's the case?" Holden asked.

"We aren't giving up," Isabel said from behind Holden. "Isn't that what you told me? You want to help people? Why would you stay here if you can help someone?"

"I wouldn't." Holden scowled at her.

"But if we get killed trying to save someone, it defeats the purpose," Spencer said.

Isabel moved closer to Holden. He felt her body heat on his side and smelled the spicy scent of her perfume. He hated that his body reacted to her. On a primal level, he was still drawn to her. He didn't want to be, but his body didn't always agree with that.

"We need to be smart. I'm not just a pretty face, boys." Isabel grinned widely, then sashayed away.

Holden resisted watching her go.

"She's a piece of work," Spencer whispered.

"Yeah, but she's good at what she does," Donahue said.

"She's batshit crazy," Spencer said. "And she's trying to get her claws back in my partner here."

"You two called it quits?" Donahue asked.

"He's got a thing for Mackenzie."

"Dude!" Holden hissed.

"Mackenzie? From the call center?" Donahue asked.

"Yep," Spencer said.

Donahue looked Holden up and down, then nodded approvingly. "I can see that. Mackenzie is a smart and strong. She's had some shit in her life, though. Don't fuck with her."

Spencer snorted. "He definitely won't fuck *with* her. He might—"

"Okay, time to go," Holden said, dragging his partner away as Spencer and Donahue laughed. "What the hell?"

Spencer chuckled. "Relax. Donahue likes Mackenzie. He's not going to say anything. He doesn't gossip like the young kids. Us old men are beyond shit like that."

"Says the man who just gossiped about me while I was standing next to you."

"Not gossip if you were there. Plus, it's the truth."

Holden scowled again. He couldn't think of an argument, so he just ignored his partner and headed for the weight room.

Where he found Isabel.

"I figured you'd find me again. Want to work out together?" Isabel said, setting down the hand weights she was using and approaching him.

"No. I'll come back another time."

Isabel chased after him into the hallway. "Holden, wait. We're going to be here for days together. We should at least be able to get along."

"We get along fine, Isabel."

"Really?" She tossed her hair over her shoulder and stepped closer. She looked up at him with those seductive eyes of hers. She was beautiful, but he knew who she really was inside. And inside was what mattered to him.

Holden had been told his entire life that he was nothing more than a pretty face, and he was done using that. He was done believing that. And he was done associating with others who were like that. He wanted more for himself. He wanted something that mattered. A relationship that was about more than arm candy. Whether he was the arm candy or not.

"Yeah," Holden said. "We're good."

"So then, why are you running away?"

"I'm not running. Just have somewhere else I need to be."

Holden walked away before she could come up with another argument. He was almost looking forward to being there for a few days, especially once he found out Mackenzie was working, too, but with Isabel around, the excitement wore off in a hurry.

Holden went back to the bay. There was always work to be done there. Two guys were doing inventory, and another pair was restocking the back of one of the ambulances. Holden asked if they needed any help just as the alarm went off.

"We're up," Riley, one of the guys from the first pair, said. He jumped in their rig as Hammer, his partner, hit the button to roll up the door in front of them.

"Fuck, that's cold," Hammer said.

"Get in," Holden told him. "I'll close it."

"Thanks, man."

The ambulance rolled out slowly, the snow outside crunching under their tires. When they were clear, Holden hit the button for the door to close, shivering against the snow piling inside.

The lights on the ambulance disappeared far too quickly. It was getting bad outside. Worse than just an hour earlier when Holden and Spencer made their last trip.

Holden grabbed a broom and swept the snow that flew inside toward the drain. Then he grabbed his coat and a shovel and headed outside.

Wind whipped around him. His hood refused to stay up. His hands were almost frozen through his gloves in minutes. It was bitterly cold outside, a cold that was only made worse by the wind throwing snow around.

Holden couldn't see far, but he could tell the snowblower had been driven over the pad in front of the building not long ago. The sidewalks were covered, so he started there.

The snow was deep and heavy. Almost a foot had piled up since the last time the sidewalks were cleared. They were all doing what they could to keep the building accessible, but it was snowing fast.

Holden listened to the wind as he worked. No vehicles passed on the road. Besides the wind, it was quiet.

Holden made it to the end of the sidewalk and took a break. He was warm, sweaty, and out of breath. And it looked as though he hadn't done a damn thing. The snow was falling so fast, where he started was already covered again.

"Fuck," Holden breathed. He could stay out there all day and shovel the sidewalk, or he could go back inside and see if there were any updates on the storm.

"We're grounded," Spencer said as soon as Holden walked in.

"What do you mean, grounded? We don't get grounded."

Spencer shook his head. "Riley and Hammer just left. They're stuck."

"What? I just saw them. I closed the door for them. Stuck? Where? How?"

"They called it in. Said they got halfway to the call and stopped dead in the road. The plows haven't been out and they can't get through the snow."

"What are they going to do?"

Spencer shook his head slowly.

"What does that mean? Why are you just shaking your head?"

"They're stuck. They can't go anywhere. There are cars blocking all the roads. Plows can't get through, and they can't keep up with all the snow, anyway. They need trucks to haul the snow away, but they don't have enough support to manage a storm like this. Command isn't letting anyone else leave."

"What if people need help?"

"We're each being assigned an operator to work with. We're going to help them talk any callers through whatever they need."

"We're gonna do what?"

"I signed you up to work with Mackenzie. You're her partner for today."

Holden was starting to like the plan. Until he remembered the last time he saw Mackenzie, she threw herself at him, then ran off.

"I'm not sure she's going to be so happy about that."

"Too late because everyone is assigned. Let's go."

MACKENZIE STARED at her screen and tried not to throw up. She couldn't believe how many calls had come in over the years with the name Damon attached to them. Sure, it might not be the same Damon, but she had to consider the possibility it was.

She was reading through a transcription from three years ago when someone next to her said, "Hey."

Mackenzie jumped, looking up at Holden. She hadn't seen him since she kissed him and ran away. He was standing over her, far too tempting for her sanity.

"I'm your partner for the day," Holden said, still smiling at her.

"Oh, um, okay." Mackenzie clicked her screen, closing the transcription before he could see what she was reading.

She'd heard they were all getting partners, but when the other paramedics filtered in and approached other operators, Mackenzie assumed no one wanted to work with her and went back to what she was doing.

"Do you mind if I sit?" There wasn't an extra chair at her station, but there was a table right behind her. Holden grabbed a chair and dragged it over, waiting for Mackenzie to nod before he took a seat.

She focused on her screen instead of the man next to her. He was kind and thoughtful and not someone she could risk getting involved with. She'd already messed up when she kissed him, but she wouldn't make that mistake again. She had to stay focused on her job. On helping others and finding Damon Street before he killed anyone else.

"What are you doing?" Holden asked.

"Logging in to the system."

"You weren't logged in before?"

"I was following up on something," Mackenzie said. Captain Patrick said not to trust anyone, and Mackenzie was going to be sure she followed that order.

"Anything I can help with?"

"No," she blurted.

"I—"

The phone rang, and Mackenzie jumped on it before Holden could finish whatever he was going to say. "Nine-one-one, what's your emergency?"

Holden sat there while Mackenzie spoke to the person on the other end of the line. Her heart ached as the woman told Mackenzie her husband went to work that morning and hadn't checked in with her since. She was anxious and frustrated and desperate.

"There are power outages all over the area, unfortunately. Maybe his phone died and he doesn't have a way to charge it."

"He always lets me know when he gets to work. He knows I worry."

"I understand it's scary. Unfortunately, our crews are not leaving the building at this point. Our vehicles are getting stuck and we can't get out to look for people."

"You're not helping anyone? What if he's run off the road somewhere? What if he's hurt and needs help? How can you sit there and do nothing?"

"I wish there was more we could do. I'm so sorry."

"You're sorry? My husband could be dying and you're sorry?"

These were the times Mackenzie hated her job. When her hands were tied and she was out of options. "If I had the authority to send a crew out to look for him, I would, but the order came from our bosses."

"Fine. Thanks for nothing."

"I'm sorry. I hope he checks in with you. Stay safe."

The woman hung up without another word. Mackenzie wanted to cry. She felt the same frustration as the woman. She hung up the phone and tried not to let Holden see how defeated she felt.

"Have they all been like that?" Holden asked softly.

Mackenzie nodded. "People are scared. They're worried about their loved ones. Some haven't come home, some didn't make it to work. I had one caller who was having a panic attack because she wasn't sure how she was going to walk her dog and when she got outside, the dog took off and she couldn't find it. It's horrible."

"Shit. I can't imagine. This is going to be hard."

Mackenzie nodded again. "Yep."

The phone rang, and Mackenzie reached for it. Holden

sat next to her, his presence making her feel both vulnerable and stronger.

It was someone else looking for a loved one. This man's wife ran out to the grocery store for last-minute things. He was tracking her location and could see where she was, and it wasn't at the grocery store. Again, Mackenzie had to tell him no one was allowed out, and again, he was angry. As the call went on, Mackenzie grew more and more upset. When she finally hung up, she took a breath, but the phone rang almost immediately.

She did her best to console everyone she spoke to. Her patience was wearing thin, but she knew the callers were scared, not angry. They needed help, and she couldn't give it to them. It was a feeling she'd never had before when sitting at that desk. She always had advice. She could tell them someone was on the way. She could help. Until today.

After an hour of endless calls, Holden shifted toward her and said, "Sign off for a minute. I need a break."

"You can go. I'll keep answering calls."

"I thought you were required to take breaks regularly."

She nodded once, reluctantly.

"How long have you been answering calls?"

"There are lots of people who need help."

"Mack, five minutes. Just take five minutes."

She sucked in a breath and looked up at him. She nibbled her lower lip and pushed her glasses up, then nodded. "Okay."

Holden waited while she logged out of the system and locked her computer. When she got up, he followed her, going to the break room to get a snack and a cup of coffee.

"I need to run to the restroom, but I'll be right back. Stay here," Holden implored.

Mackenzie nodded and watched him go. She debated

going back to her desk and signing in again, but she was exhausted. A break was a good idea.

"Holden and I snuck into the closet the other day. It was hot. And being here together... Let's just say if you hear something from one of the storage rooms, don't come in." Isabel and Eric walked into the break room, heads together. Isabel grinned like she had a secret, even though she just told Eric everything.

"He's so sexy," Eric said with a shiver. "I don't know how you snagged him, but you're damn lucky."

"I know. But we have to keep quiet about it. He doesn't like everyone knowing. He's a rule follower. He's always worried we're going to get caught fucking in a closet or something."

Eric zipped his lips and grinned.

The two of them finally looked up from each other and saw Mackenzie. Isabel gave Mackenzie a self-satisfied smirk, and Eric just grinned kindly.

"Hey, Mackenzie. I didn't see you. How's it going? These calls are rough, right?" Eric said, talking a mile a minute like he was nervous.

"Yeah, they are."

"Who are you paired with?" Eric asked.

"Holden Cross," Mackenzie said.

Eric gasped, his lips curling up in a grin as he looked back at a scowling Isabel. "Holden's a nice guy. I'm sure he's very capable."

"He definitely is," Isabel said in a sugar-coated voice. "He's always nice to everyone. Would never say a nasty thing...to someone's face. He's far too kind for that."

Mackenzie nodded. She swallowed roughly. Holden was nice to her, but she never realized it was only to her face.

Mackenzie's throat got tight, and she struggled to choke down the rest of her coffee.

"Well, we're just working together. It's not like we're looking for closets to fuck in or anything. I'll leave that to you." Mackenzie threw her coffee away and shoved the door open. She stomped back to her desk and flopped onto her chair. Her cheeks burned with shame. She hadn't met Isabel many times, but they'd never had a nasty relationship. Mackenzie had no idea why Isabel seemed to hate her all of a sudden.

Holden must have told Isabel that Mackenzie kissed him. They must have laughed about it. He probably said he was lucky to be alive after being alone with her.

She was so stupid. She thought he was a good guy. Decent. Kind. She couldn't have been more wrong about him.

Mackenzie slid her headset on and was about to login to the system when Holden took his seat next to her.

"I thought you were going to take a break."

Mackenzie shook her head, fighting tears. "I had enough of a break. You can go, though. Find someone else to work with. I know you were stuck with me and don't really want to be near me."

"What? That's not true. I want to be here."

"Just stop," Mackenzie said, losing her battle against her tears. "I know about Isabel. And I'm not looking to be someone's pawn or something. I don't even know what you're doing. No one around here would ever actually believe you might like me, so you can stop using me to make her jealous or whatever. Find a closet and get it over with so I can do my job."

"What are you talking about?"

Mackenzie stared at him. He was good. She almost

thought he was clueless. But she'd been fooled enough times in her life. She wasn't falling for it again.

"I'm going to go to the bathroom. While I'm gone, find a closet for you and Isabel or find someone else to work with. I don't really care. Just don't be here when I get back."

5

—————

MACKENZIE WALKED AWAY, NOT CARING THAT HE WAS CALLING her name. She pushed her way into the bathroom. It was empty, giving her a minute to compose herself. She dried her tears and sucked in a few deep breaths, fighting her emotions.

It was going to be a long few days if she was going to let them get to her. She had to push it all down. She could feel her feelings when she was away from everyone. But for now, she had to pull herself together.

Mackenzie walked out of the bathroom and saw Isabel leaving the break room. Isabel stopped in the hallway, talking to Eric and blocking the way back to the call center. Mackenzie couldn't just stand there and hope they didn't notice her. She had to leave.

She turned toward the paramedic side of the building. A long hallway connected the two buildings. Mackenzie didn't think about where she was going, just walked down the hallway until she came to another door.

She pushed inside and was greeted by quiet. Blissful, peaceful silence. She could finally breathe.

Mackenzie leaned against the wall and inhaled deep. With all the paramedics on her side of the building, it was empty, and she could enjoy the silence. She needed the break. From Holden and Isabel and everyone. Taking calls for days without a break was going to be bad enough, but doing it with Holden hovering over her shoulder was going to be painful. Especially knowing he was only there with her because he had no other choice.

Mackenzie finally breathed normally. The quiet echoed around her, the wind howling outside the building. The ambulances were eerily quiet in the bays, no banging or sirens or anything. It could have been creepy, but Mackenzie enjoyed the hell out of it.

Until she heard boots coming down the hall. Dammit.

Mackenzie hurried away from the door, looking for a place to hide. She found a dark office and slipped inside, hoping whoever was coming would bypass her and never know she was there. She pressed herself to the wall behind the door, doing her best to stay out of sight.

"Mackenzie," Holden called out.

Shit.

"I know you're in here. I saw you come this way. What's going on?"

"Go away, Holden," Mackenzie snapped.

His footsteps approached. She should have kept her mouth shut.

"Talk to me, Mack. Please."

He stopped outside the door. Whether it was because he knew where she was and was giving her the chance to go to him or it was because he wasn't sure where she was, Mackenzie didn't know. If she was lucky, he'd give up on her.

"What happened, Mackenzie? Why do you think I got *stuck* with you?"

"Because you did," Mackenzie breathed.

Holden stepped into the office, and then he was right there in front of her. He wasn't blocking the door, but he was in front of it, making Mackenzie feel both safe and trapped.

"Why do you think that?"

"It doesn't matter, Holden. I can handle my own calls. You can find someone to switch off with. Like Isabel."

"Isabel?" he asked, his tone cautious.

Mackenzie shrugged. "I know you'd much rather work with her."

"No, actually I wouldn't. I—"

Holden broke off his sentence when a loud boom echoed through the building. His eyes went wide, then he looked out into the bay.

"What was that?" Mackenzie asked.

"I don't know. Stay here."

"I'm not staying here. Why would I stay here? Do you think I can't take care of myself?"

"Mackenzie, I don't know what that was or—"

Another boom. Different since they were in the wide open bay where the sound bounced around.

"It sounds like someone's at the door," Mackenzie said. She pushed past Holden and headed for the exterior door.

"Mackenzie wait," Holden shouted, but Mackenzie was already on the other side of the ambulance and saw a figure leaning against the door.

"There's someone out there," Mackenzie shouted, racing toward the door. She pushed open the interior door, with Holden right behind her.

"Holy shit," Holden breathed.

The woman collapsed toward them when Holden got the door open. He barely caught her, sinking to the floor with her when she fell.

Mackenzie helped him pull her inside and closed the door behind her, making sure it was secure before she turned her attention back to the woman. Her brown skin was a gray tone, with bright red raw spots on her hands. Her lips were closer to blue. She was in jeans and a pretty top, but no jacket, gloves, or hat. She wore black heels that were definitely not meant for snow.

"What the hell was she doing outside?" Holden hissed.

Mackenzie was wondering the same thing until she saw the woman's necklace. "Edie."

"Do you know her?" Holden asked, looking between Mackenzie and Edie.

Mackenzie shook her head as her heart raced. She was alive. Mackenzie couldn't believe it. She needed to call Captain Patrick. Edie was alive.

"We need to get her inside. Get her warm," Holden said. His voice was calm, firm. He stood, lifting Edie under her arms, looping his hands beneath her breasts and catching his wrists to keep his grip secure. "Can you get her feet?"

Mackenzie shook her head and snapped out of her fog. She grabbed Edie's ankles and lifted, moving with Holden into the ambulance bay.

"Let's get her in the back of a rig. We can warm her there."

Mackenzie nodded. They moved to the closest ambulance. Mackenzie set her feet down and shouldered Edie's weight while Holden opened the back of the ambulance. He climbed in and pulled the gurney out before helping Mackenzie get Edie onto it. They pushed it back into the ambulance and closed the doors against the cool air of the wide open bay.

"She needs to be warmed up slowly so she doesn't go into shock. Her clothes are soaked. We need to get them off.

Then we can cover her with blankets and warm her up. You don't have to be here for this if you don't want to. I don't want to cause you more pain watching someone you know..."

Mackenzie's gaze snapped to Holden's. He didn't come out and say it, but he didn't think Edie was going to survive. Tears welled in Mackenzie's eyes. She couldn't accept that. They had to save her. Penny died only five days earlier, and Mackenzie was sure Edie was close to death because of Damon, too. She was not going to let him take another woman's life.

"I'm not leaving her."

Holden nodded once, then went to work cutting off Edie's clothes. He left on her bra and panties, but the rest was cut to pieces and carefully removed. When he got one piece of clothing off, he covered her in a blanket and put room temperature water bottles next to her.

"They'd be better if they were warm, but it's better than nothing," Holden said.

Everything he did, he explained to Mackenzie. When he needed her help, he asked for it. Mackenzie followed each of Holden's instructions. They worked together for an hour before Edie finally started to look a little less dead. She was breathing better, and she'd stopped shivering.

"We can try to take the oxygen mask off of her," Holden said quietly. The entire place was so quiet that speaking above a whisper felt like shouting.

"What do you think?" Mackenzie asked.

Holden looked at the monitor. "Let's give her a little longer. I think she's doing well, but it won't hurt to leave her on it. The truck has plenty."

Mackenzie sat on the bench next to Edie and held her hand. She dreaded having to tell the woman that her cousin was dead, but that wasn't a problem for the moment. First, Edie needed to survive.

"How do you know Edie?" Holden asked after another hour of staring at her and checking her vitals.

Mackenzie kept stroking the other woman's hand, not daring to look away in case something happened. "I don't know her."

"You said her name. You've never met?"

Mackenzie shook her head. "It's on her necklace."

"Oh. The way you said it sounded like..."

"I know *of* her," Mackenzie admitted.

"Of her? How?"

Mackenzie took a deep breath and stared at the woman's face. It was easier than looking at Holden. "Do you remember the press conference from last week? About the woman who supposedly killed her friend but didn't and the friend was alive but another woman was dead?"

Holden chuckled. "Yeah. That's not something that happens often."

"Part of it," Mackenzie breathed. "Anyway, the woman who was killed was here looking for her cousin. Her cousin was missing, and no one had any leads, but she was convinced something had happened to her."

"Okay. I can understand being worried if someone disappeared."

Mackenzie nodded.

"What does that have to do with this woman?"

Mackenzie finally looked up at him. "The cousin's name was Edie."

Holden's gaze snapped to the unconscious woman lying between them. "Shit, really?"

Mackenzie looked at Edie again. "I think this might be her."

"Wow. Well, we need to let someone know. If she's missing, the police need to know she's alive." Holden made a move to get out of the ambulance, but Mackenzie stopped him.

"You can't call the police."

"Excuse me?"

"You can't call the police. They can't be trusted. I don't even know if you can be trusted. But no one can know Edie is here. Or she'll be dead before this storm is over."

HOLDEN SAT BACK DOWN on the bench and gawked at Mackenzie. She stared at Edie instead of him. "You can't be serious."

Mackenzie nodded. "I am. I have a contact that can be trusted. I'm going to tell him you're here with me. If anything happens, he'll know you were to blame."

Holden almost laughed. She honestly thought he was going to kill an innocent woman? An innocent woman who was unconscious and almost froze to death? "Is that really what you think of me?"

"I don't think anything about you, Holden. You wouldn't even know about Edie if you hadn't followed me down here. You should go back. I'm sure Isabel is wondering where you are by now."

"And why would I care what Isabel thinks?" Holden snapped. It was the second time Mackenzie mentioned Isabel.

"Because you're dating. Or at least having sex in closets. I don't know. And I don't care. It's none of my business."

"What? Who told you that?"

"Isabel. Well, she didn't tell me. She was telling Eric, but

I just happened to be there. She was talking about how you two were going to have sex in a closet while everyone was here and not to go into any if he heard noises. And it's fine. I don't care. I didn't mean to kiss you last week, anyway. And I never would have if I'd known you were involved with someone. And…" She finally looked up at him and stopped. "What?"

Holden stared at her, his mouth open and arms crossed. "Isabel is lying, and so are you."

"No, I'm not. That's what she said. Why would I make that up?"

"You're lying about not meaning to kiss me last week. You can't fake that kind of thing."

Mackenzie avoided his gaze and turned to Edie again. Even looking away, Holden saw the flush rising up her cheeks. "It was nothing. It never should have happened. I'm sorry."

"I'm not. Do you know how long I've wanted to kiss you?"

She scoffed. "Yeah, I'm sure."

He lifted her chin with his fingertip and waited until she raised her gaze to his. Her big brown eyes were wide and vulnerable, just like they'd been before she kissed him. "I have liked you for a long time, Mackenzie. But I never thought you'd be open to me asking you out or kissing you, so I've tried to be friends with you, and even that has proven to be a challenge. But when you kissed me, I couldn't stop smiling for days."

"Why?" she blurted.

"Why what?"

"Why would you be happy that I kissed you? Why would you want to be my friend? Any of it. All of it."

"You hide yourself, Mackenzie, but I see you. I see the

way you talk to callers and do everything you can to make sure they have a good outcome. I see how you go out of your way to be kind to your coworkers, even though many of them don't return that gesture. I see how you hold things in and bottle up your emotions, like you're doing right now, but you care so deeply about people that when they are hurt or in danger, you ache for them. I might not know you, Mackenzie, but I really do want to."

"But you're with Isabel."

Holden shook his head. "I'm not. I haven't been for a while. We used to date, but we want different things."

"Like what?"

Holden hesitated. He wanted to tell Mackenzie about training to be a flight paramedic, but he wasn't sure she would have a different reaction than Isabel had, so he kept his mouth shut on that one. "We just have different goals and values."

"But she's gorgeous."

Holden bristled at the way she said that, as if someone being attractive was a good enough reason to date them. "That's not enough for some people."

"It shouldn't be for anyone, but I've never known a man to turn down a woman who looks like Isabel to talk to someone like me."

"Then you haven't been paying me much attention."

Mackenzie gasped. She licked her lips, drawing the lower one between her teeth.

Edie groaned, drawing both of their attention.

"Edie?" Mackenzie whispered.

Edie opened her eyes and looked up. "Where...?"

She passed out just that quickly again.

"Edie? Is she okay? What happened?" Mackenzie's voice rose with each question.

Holden reached across and grabbed her hand. "Her body needs to rest. She will be in and out of consciousness for a while, until her body warms up. All we can do is wait."

Mackenzie exhaled slowly, her gaze not straying from Edie. "Okay."

Holden watched Mackenzie as she watched Edie for a long few moments. Edie's breathing evened out, and Mackenzie seemed to relax again finally.

"Do you want to call your contact?" Holden asked.

Mackenzie nodded, digging her phone out of her pocket. "I should."

Holden watched her as she chewed the inside of her cheek. She scrolled through her phone, then tapped the screen and lifted it to her ear.

Holden heard a man's voice answer, but he couldn't make out what he said.

"She's alive," Mackenzie whispered. Her voice shook with those two words, and her firm outer shell cracked. She sucked in a sob and lowered the phone from her ear. She heaved another breath, then raised the phone again. "Edie is at the station. I'm looking at her right now."

Mackenzie paused while the man spoke.

Mackenzie looked up at Holden. "She came to the door, and I was in the ambulance bay with Holden Cross. He's a paramedic. He's—"

She stopped when the man said something.

"I think I can trust him. I hope so."

"You can trust me," Holden said out loud, not sure and not caring if the man could hear him.

"He'd like to speak to you," Mackenzie said, offering him the phone.

Holden looked at it for a second, then took it from her,

their fingers brushing and sending a jolt through him. "Cross."

"This is Captain Marcus Patrick."

Holden lifted his gaze to Mackenzie. She didn't have a random contact. She had the personal phone number of the highest ranking person in the police department.

"Hello, sir," Holden said.

"I know we've never met, but I've heard good things about you. If you're there with Mackenzie and she trusts you, I will as well. Do not make me feel like a fool for that choice."

"No, sir."

"The woman you have, Edie. Is she going to survive?"

Holden looked at the monitor he had hooked up to Edie. "Her vitals are stable. She's still cold, but she's better than she was when she arrived. We have her in the back of an ambulance, but we're unable to get out of the building at this point to take her to the hospital."

"Are you able to keep her alive without telling anyone else what's going on?"

"I think so, but people will notice Mackenzie and I are missing after a while. Actually, I'm a little unsure why no one has come looking for us yet. It's been hours since we've been gone."

"Things are a bit crazy right now. I imagine they're all working too much to realize you're missing." Captain Patrick paused, exhaling a deep breath like he had something else to say.

Holden waited.

"We believe Edie was taken and held against her will for months by a man named Damon Street. We think his organization was able to keep her because they gave her drugs. Lots of them. I have no way of knowing why she's in your ambulance right now and not where she's been since she disappeared, but I wanted you prepared in case she was loaded up on drugs and ends up coming down while you're with her."

"We have naloxone, but that won't help unless she's overdosed. She's been in and out of consciousness, so I'm assuming we're past that point already."

"I agree," Captain Patrick said. "Unfortunately, nothing will help her. But I needed you aware so you don't give her anything that could have an adverse reaction because of the drugs."

"Any idea what kind of drugs?"

"Likely all of them. Anything they could get their hands on, which was basically anything, they likely forced on that poor woman."

"Jesus," Holden breathed.

"Yeah. Holden, please take care of both of them."

Holden looked up at Mackenzie and nodded. "I will, sir."

He handed the phone back to Mackenzie. She spoke to Captain Patrick a few more minutes, then hung up and met Holden's gaze.

"I know why no one's come looking for me, but why haven't they come looking for you?" she asked, as if just realizing herself it had been a while.

Holden shook his head, a feeling of dread sinking into his stomach. The ambulance had been getting colder and colder while they sat there, but he assumed it was just because the temperature outside was continuing to drop. The heat was only so good in the bay where the ceiling was three stories high and the insulation was mediocre.

But that didn't explain why no one had come looking for them.

"I'll be right back."

He got out of the ambulance, rubbing his hands together to fend off the cold. He moved around the room, finding nothing that would explain what was going on. He got to the door to the hallway and stopped. There was snow underneath the door. And daylight on the other side.

The hallway had collapsed. They were trapped.

6

———

Mackenzie stared at Edie with a mixture of fear and relief. Edie was alive, but just like Penny, she'd been left out in the cold. How she ended up at the station, Mackenzie didn't know.

Now that she was warming up, Makenzie saw bruises on Edie's face. Mackenzie's stomach turned at the thought of where else the woman might have bruises and what other trauma she'd been through.

Mackenzie rubbed her hands together and blew into them. She was getting cold. Strange, since the building was insulated and heated, but she figured it was because the bay was so huge. Being in the ambulance was a good idea, but it was too bad they couldn't turn it on and warm up.

A few minutes passed, and Holden didn't return. Mackenzie started to wonder if he'd left and told someone about Edie. If he was bringing back an accomplice to help him kill both of them.

Mackenzie looked around the ambulance and tried to figure out what she could use as a weapon. If Holden was going to try to kill her, she wasn't going down without a fight. She opened one cabinet after another, finding nothing sharp or deadly. She was pretty sure gauze bandages wouldn't hold him and wouldn't do much good. Not until after he attacked her.

The door opened, and Mackenzie screamed and jumped and whirled around, holding a roll of sterile tape out toward Holden.

Holden climbed into the ambulance and closed the doors before he looked up at her. "What's that for?"

"I got worried because you were gone so long. I thought... Never mind."

He narrowed his eyes at her and looked around at the open cabinets and supplies strewn all over. "You thought I was going to come back with a weapon."

"No. Maybe. Yes. And a partner since there are two of us."

"Well, Edie's not putting up much of a fight, and I took this job to help people, not hurt them, so you're safe. Both of you. Sort of."

Mackenzie felt better until he said that last part. "Sort of? What does that mean?"

Holden settled against the side of the ambulance and rubbed his hands together. He blew into them like Mackenzie had done just minutes earlier and looked around. "We can't stay here."

"We can't take her to the call center. It's too risky."

Holden shook his head. "It's also blocked."

"What?"

He blew out a breath slowly and met Mackenzie's gaze. "The hallway collapsed. That's why no one's come looking for us."

"What are you talking about?"

"That first sound we heard must have been the hallway.

It's a flat roof, and with the amount of snow we have, all of it piled on top was too much. It caved in. There's no way we can get to the other side. Snow is already coming in through the door and the hallway is completely blocked. I was trying to see if we could get through, that's what took me so long, but between the debris from the collapse and the snow, it's not possible. We're stuck on this side."

"You're kidding me. There's no way," Mackenzie shrieked, panic rising inside her. She scrambled to the ambulance door and flung it open, ignoring that it was noticeably colder outside the vehicle. She raced to the door that she came through hours ago. Her escape, where she ran to avoid Holden's girlfriend, and Holden, was a wall of mangled metal and snow.

She grabbed a piece of something and tugged. Her hands were cold on the frozen metal, but she didn't stop pulling. She screamed and yanked, changing position and pulling on something else, but nothing moved more than an inch or two, then went right back to where it was when she let go.

Frustrated, angry tears rolled down Mackenzie's face. She was vaguely aware that Holden was standing behind her, but she couldn't care at the moment. She needed to get out of there. She needed to be on the other side. To help people who were trapped in the storm and needed her. To not be alone with a man who made her want things she had no business wanting. Ever. It wasn't safe. Holden wasn't safe. Not for her heart because the stupid organ wanted more.

Mackenzie collapsed to the ground and sobbed. She stared at the mess and screamed into the whipping wind and mocking metal and prayed to whatever entity would listen to help her.

"I'm sorry, Mack. I should have checked hours ago. Then we wouldn't be trapped here."

Mackenzie looked up at him and wiped the tears from her face. When his eyes went wide and he lunged for her, she withdrew in fear.

"You're bleeding," he gasped, pausing when he saw the look in her eyes. "Please, let me see. You must have cut your hands."

Mackenzie flipped her hands over and sucked in a breath. They didn't even hurt, but they were sliced in multiple places and oozing blood from all the cuts.

Holden gingerly took her hands in his and examined one, then the other. "We need to get you bandaged up, then we all need to get upstairs. It'll be warmer up there."

Mackenzie nodded, knowing he was right. Her frustration would have to wait. She couldn't do anything about where they were or who she was trapped with. At least she knew they had plenty of bandages.

Holden held her hand palm up as they walked back to the ambulance. He'd closed the doors, but it was still cold inside. Edie hadn't moved. Mackenzie looked at her again and prayed she'd survive. Prayed they all would.

Holden grabbed gauze and bandages and antiseptic spray from the cabinets overhead. He shoved all the supplies into a bag near the door, then went through more cabinets and took out vials of medicine, a few syringes, and bags of fluids. Everything went into the bag at the door, then he held it out to Mackenzie.

"Can I put this over your shoulder? I'll carry Edie upstairs, but if you can carry that, it'll be a huge help. If not, I can make two trips."

Mackenzie shook her head and reached for the bag. "I can do it."

"Let me put it on you," Holden said, pulling the bag away from her. "I don't want you to irritate your wounds or to risk getting any fibers in them. I'm going to lift it over your head, and you can raise one arm."

She did as he said, the bag resting on her shoulder. It was awkward across her body with the bag at her side instead of behind her.

"Is that okay?" Holden asked.

"It's fine."

"I don't want you adjusting it, so if you need me to move it so it's more comfortable, let me know now."

"I'd rather have it at my back to walk up the stairs." Mackenzie didn't look at him. She didn't want to explain to him that when she climbed stairs, her hips were wide and a bag could catch on something, or just rub the edge of the stairs. It also made her feel off balance, and if she couldn't use her hands, she was afraid she might fall.

"Sorry," Hold said. "I should have thought of that. I'm going to grab the bag and lift. I need to adjust the strap." He swallowed hard and lifted the weight of the bag.

The strap across Mackenzie's front drooped, catching on her breast. She reached up to move it, but stopped herself before she touched it.

Holden lifted the strap at her back and eased it forward as he slid the bag to her back. When he had it positioned behind her, he slowly lowered the bag, letting her carry the weight of it again. The strap nestled between her breasts and pulled tight across her rounded belly.

"Is that okay?" Holden asked, moving around her to look at her front.

Mackenzie nodded. "It's fine."

"Are you sure? I can adjust it." His gaze fell to her breasts and stayed there for a moment. Then he cleared his throat and looked away.

Mackenzie tried not to let it get to her. He was male, which meant he was wired to look at a woman's boobs. Hers were big, like all her other parts, but they were nothing like Isabel's. They weren't perky and on a platter. They were just sort of there, under her top and held up by industrial strength underwire.

"I'm good." Mackenzie shivered, the cold sinking in and the pain starting to make itself known.

"I'll get Edie. You can start up those stairs. The bunk room is up there and a few offices, and the kitchen and bathrooms. Plus, since the rooms are smaller, we'll be able to stay warm even though this side is no longer safe from the elements."

Mackenzie nodded and started toward the stairs. She took a few steps and looked back at Holden. He had Edie in his arms with the blankets wrapped all around her body. He nudged the doors closed with his hip, being careful to keep Edie secure.

Mackenzie regretted doubting him, even for a minute. He'd always been kind to her, unlike most people who worked with them. Holden was nice to look at, but he was also a nice man. Someone who seemed to care.

His lips were moving like he was whispering something to Edie as he carried her closer to Mackenzie. Mackenzie started up the stairs, knowing she wouldn't be able to go too quickly. She was halfway there when Holden caught up to her.

"Sorry I'm slow," she said.

"You're good. I'd rather you go slow than risk having to grab onto the handrail and hurt your hands even more."

"But you're carrying a person and you're faster than me."

"I do this all the time."

"Carry women upstairs at work?"

He snorted. "Definitely not that. I just meant climb these stairs. I can do it blindfolded. I've definitely done it so tired I felt like I was blindfolded."

"How long have you been working here?" Mackenzie asked for something to say.

"Almost ten years. I've been stationed at a few other places, but this one stuck. I like it here."

"So do I," Mackenzie admitted. "I tried working other places, but... It never worked out."

"Why's that?"

Mackenzie swallowed the pain she always felt when she thought about Jaclyn. Mackenzie was throwing herself a pity party because her best friend was dead. She still had a life. She could go out and do things. Jaclyn was gone forever.

"When people recognize me, it's not good for business. Being here, no one sees me, so it's easy."

"Shit, Mack, I'm sorry. I never thought about that."

They made it to the top of the stairs, and Mackenzie paused.

"To the right," Holden said, sounding slightly out of breath. "First door is a bunk room. We'll get Edie settled in there first, then we'll work on getting your hands bandaged up. You okay with that?"

"Yes, please. She's more important."

"Not to me," Holden said.

Mackenzie didn't say anything as Holden moved to a bed and laid Edie gently on it. He made sure the blankets were wrapped around her again and put his fingers to her neck.

"I couldn't bring the monitors up with me, but I think she's okay without them. I'll check her vitals manually until she wakes up."

"Sounds good."

Holden turned to Mackenzie and nodded to her hands. "Let's see what we can do about you."

Mackenzie sucked in a breath and nodded back. "Okay."

"The bathroom is through there. We need to wash your hands well, then I'll spray them and wrap them. But I want to make sure we don't risk infection. I grabbed some antibiotics just in case, but hopefully you don't need them."

Mackenzie led the way to the bathroom and looked around. There were showers in stalls on one side, and toilets on the other side with a wall of sinks in the middle of the open space. Gray tile ran from the floor up to shoulder-height on the wall with white paint above. The countertops were the same gray, and the stall doors were, too. It was very bland.

"This is probably going to sting, but you need to wash your hands. Do you want me to help?" Holden said.

Mackenzie shook her head and focused on the sink in front of her. Holden turned the water on and held out a bottle of soap. She lifted her palms to him and winced when he squirted two globs of liquid soap into her hands.

"Sorry. I hate that you're in pain. I should have stopped you."

Mackenzie shook her head and dipped her hands under the warm water. Bubbles formed as she rubbed her hands together, the shredded skin between them causing her breath to falter. "You couldn't have stopped me. I was pretty upset."

"I'm so sorry, Mack. I really am. I know you don't want to be here with me."

Mackenzie shook her head. "There are a lot of people I'd be much more unhappy to be stuck with. At least you're nice to me."

Holden caught her gaze. His eyes dilated, his chest rising and falling slowly. "I like you, Mackenzie. Being nice to you is definitely not a hardship."

She chuckled softly. "Maybe not for you."

"Definitely not for me."

Did he get closer? Mackenzie wouldn't have to move far to press her lips to his again. To kiss him one more time.

But she couldn't. She shouldn't. She moved back, forcing her focus to her hands and the bloody bubbles covering them.

"Shit. I guess you're still bleeding," Holden said. "Rinse your hands and wash them again. Try to get as much blood off as possible."

Mackenzie did as he asked and had pinkish bubbles instead of red. Holden declared her good enough and dried her hands with a gentleness she never expected from him.

"Are you okay?" he asked, his voice low and rough.

"I'm fine."

He held one hand and sprayed the antiseptic spray over it.

Mackenzie hissed in a breath, but it died when Holden raised her hand to his lips and blew a soft, cool, soothing breath over her hand.

"Is that better?"

She nodded, not trusting her voice.

He examined her hand closely, holding it up to his face and inspecting it like it held secrets of something. When he finally lowered it, he smiled at her. "No shards of metal or anything that I can see. If you feel a sharp pain in any of these cuts at any point, let me know immediately because I could have missed something."

Mackenzie nodded again.

Holden did the same thing with her other hand, and

again, Mackenzie lost her ability to speak when he blew on her hand. He wrapped that one up just like the first, until she felt like a mummy.

"I don't think I can even feed myself with this much gauze on my hands."

"You're lucky you didn't cut your fingers. And you should be able to hold a spoon or something. Or I'll have to feed you."

Mackenzie had a flash of herself on her knees in front of Holden, sucking on his cock. She sucked in a ragged breath and pressed her thighs together. She could not start thinking about him like that. Not when he was being nice. Not ever.

Holden threw away all the used supplies from her bandages and cleaned up the sink area, then said he was going to check on Edie.

Mackenzie followed him to the bunk room, thankful Edie was still sleeping. She wasn't sure what they would do if she needed more medical attention than they were able to provide there, but she believed Holden would do everything possible to save Edie.

"Should we find something to eat?" Holden asked.

"Yes, but we should also probably tell someone what happened. Can you call Isabel or someone?"

Holden shook his head. "I don't have my phone. I left it on your desk when I followed you down here. I was looking at something, then saw you come down the hall and set it down without thinking."

"I don't have a number for anyone," Mackenzie said. "I'm not really friends with my coworkers."

Holden looked at her with a kind smile. "They're the ones missing out. But I guess we know why no one's tried to contact us."

"Yeah, I guess. Do you know any phone numbers for anyone over there?"

Holden shook his head. "Not by heart. Can we call nine-one-one?"

Mackenzie shrugged. "I guess it's our best option."

"Call first, then food."

HOLDEN CRINGED when Eric answered their call. Mackenzie had the phone on speaker so they could both talk to whoever answered, but he wished she hadn't when Eric picked up.

"Oh, my God, Mackenzie, where are you?"

"I'm trapped on the paramedic side of the building. The hallway collapsed when I was over here."

"What were you doing over there? You have no right to be there," Isabel snapped. "You—"

"She's here with me," Holden said, putting a stop to whatever nasty thing Isabel was going to say to Mackenzie. He was not going to allow Isabel to be mean.

"Holden? I've been so worried about you, baby. I thought you were trapped in the hallway, but this is worse."

"Being trapped with a perfectly nice woman is worse than me being trapped under a collapsed roof and exposed to the half a dozen feet of snow we're getting?"

"She's a murderer," Isabel hissed, like that meant Mackenzie wouldn't hear her.

Holden looked up at Mackenzie and caught the pain on her face before she looked away. She made a move to stand, but Holden grabbed her wrist and held her there. "Mackenzie is no more a murderer than I am. She's kind and generous and beautiful."

Isabel scoffed.

"And you and I are not together and we're never going to be back together, Isabel, so please stop telling people we're going to be fucking around while we're both trapped here. Even if I wasn't stuck on the other side of the building from you, there's no way in hell that would happen. I told you we're done."

Isabel squeaked, and a loud bang echoed through the phone.

"Um, she had to go. Are you two okay?" Eric asked.

"We're fine," Holden said. "We have food and a bathroom and places to sleep. We'll be okay. Just hate that we can't be over on that side helping people."

"Your job now is to keep each other occupied. Mackenzie, you good?"

Holden looked at Mackenzie. She avoided his gaze, but she leaned toward the phone. "I'm fine."

"Ignore Isabel, hun. She's just jealous. You two be careful over there."

"Thanks, Eric."

"Bye."

They hung up with Eric and looked at each other. The moment was heavy with tension, and Holden wanted nothing more than to lean in and kiss Mackenzie, but before he had the chance, she pulled back and stood.

"We should get something to eat."

Holden nodded, even though she couldn't see him. She was already gone. In the kitchen, away from him.

7

HOLDEN HUNG BACK WHILE MACKENZIE WENT THROUGH THE fridge and the cabinets in the kitchen. There was always plenty of food there, but she apparently didn't like the options.

Mackenzie slammed a cabinet closed and leaned against the counter, her bandaged hands hovering over the surface. She drew in a slow, deep breath, then blew it out again. She did it twice more, then closed her eyes and did it a third time.

"You can go out the front door and make it to the call center. You don't have to stay here with me," Mackenzie said softly.

"Why would I do that?"

"So you aren't stuck here with a suspected killer."

Holden laughed, which got him a glare from Mackenzie.

"You don't have to laugh at me," she whispered. Her lip wobbled for half a second before she pulled it between her teeth. It turned white next to where she bit down.

Holden moved across the room to her side. He was sure it was the wrong time to put his hands on her, but he couldn't resist any longer. He pulled her into his arms, even as she tried to push him away, and held her.

Mackenzie stood there, unmoving, for a full minute.

Holden just waited. If she pushed him off again, he'd let her go, but he had the feeling she needed to know he was there.

Just when he was about to release her, Mackenzie's arms went around his waist. A soft sob escaped her, followed by a full body tremor that made Holden's gut twist.

Mackenzie held onto him and cried quietly. She didn't speak or collapse or fall apart, but she did lean on him, giving him her weight and wrapping her arms around him in a way that had him hardening.

Not the time, he told his cock, trying to stop it from rising and letting Mackenzie know he was getting turned on while she was upset.

Mackenzie drew a deep breath and released it with a shudder, then eased her arms from around him. She took a step back, avoiding his gaze for a moment while she wiped her tears with the backs of her hands. When she looked up at him, the sadness in her eyes gutted him.

"Thank you. But I meant what I said."

"And I meant what I didn't say just now. I'm here for you, Mack. I know you didn't kill your friend. You're kind and thoughtful and amazing. You'd never hurt someone."

"Most people don't believe that."

"Most people don't know you."

"You don't know me."

Holden shook his head. "Maybe not as well as I'd like, but people don't get into this kind of work if they don't care about others."

"I might argue that point concerning your girlfriend."

Holden chuckled. "Isabel is a piece of work. Also, my ex-girlfriend."

Mackenzie held his gaze for a long moment, then nodded. She stared at Holden, like she couldn't believe he was there.

He didn't look away, letting her see whatever it was she wanted to see. She'd been forced into trusting him, but more than anything, he wanted her to actually trust him. To tell him what was going on. To lean on him and know he'd be there for her. No matter what.

"We should get some food. I'm sure Edie will be hungry when she wakes up."

Holden nodded, letting her look through the cabinets again. When she still came up empty, he stepped forward and offered to make something.

"Do you cook?"

"I do. Rather well, I think. Why don't you go sit with Edie for a few minutes and I'll get something started."

Mackenzie exhaled heavily and nodded.

Without her in the kitchen, Holden felt like he could think clearly again. He went through the cabinets and fridge and freezer and decided soup was a good option. And it was something they could eat more than once. There were frozen rolls and plenty of things to add to a hearty chicken soup, and he got to work.

Mackenzie came back in when Holden had everything in the stockpot and was stirring the mixture. The oven was almost preheated, so he had rolls lined up on a sheet pan, ready to go in.

"It smells good in here," Mackenzie said.

Holden grinned. "Thanks. Chicken soup is easy, but it always hits the spot. Rolls and extra noodles to make sure it's filling enough."

Mackenzie looked around. "Is there anything I can do?"

Holden shook his head as the oven beeped to let him know it was preheated. He slid the rolls in and closed the door. "All set. It should be ready in about twenty minutes."

"Bowls? Silverware? Anything like that I can get out?"

"Sure. Upper cabinet over there." Holden paused, unsure if he should talk to Mackenzie about Edie and her potential withdrawal. It could get very ugly. Even though she heard his side of the conversation with Captain Patrick, Holden didn't know how much Mackenzie knew about what Edie was facing. "How's Edie doing?"

"I think okay. Her skin is finally almost warm, and she seems to be breathing okay. I'm guessing she'll start to go through drug withdrawal at some point, but I'm not sure how long before something like that happens, or how long it's been since she had anything."

"I've been wondering about that, too. I wasn't sure if you wanted to talk about it."

Mackenzie looked up at him. "Have you ever treated someone during a withdrawal?"

"No. Usually we get them when they're high. They go to the hospital and the people there are the ones responsible for withdrawal. That or rehab."

Mackenzie stared off beyond Holden. "Is it something that can kill her?"

Holden shook his head. "No. It shouldn't be. But it's going to be miserable for her. She's going to want to claw her skin off."

"How do we stop her from doing that?"

"Unfortunately, I don't really know."

MACKENZIE SAT opposite Holden at the table and ate her soup, thankful she could use the spoon without too much trouble with her bandaged hands. The soup was warm and delicious and perfect for their evening. She realized as she was eating that she hadn't had anything in hours and was starving.

When they were finished, Holden put the rest of the soup in a large container and put it in the fridge. He carried a small bowl of broth to Edie and tried to get her to eat something.

She parted her lips when the spoon touched them and swallowed the broth. He fed her a little more, but it wasn't long before Edie was asleep again and not eating.

Mackenzie pressed her bandaged hands together, the reality of her situation sinking in. She was going to be spending the night with a drug addict and a man she didn't know very well. If anything happened, she was completely alone. Captain Patrick knew where she was and what was going on, but that didn't mean she'd survive the night.

"You doing okay?" Holden asked softly.

Mackenzie forced a smile and looked up toward him, not meeting his gaze. "Yeah. All good."

"Are you worried about Edie going through withdrawal?"

Mackenzie nodded.

"But that's not it, is it? Are you worried about me? Do you think I'm going to do something? Shit. I'm sorry. I will stay away. I never even thought—"

"It's not you," Mackenzie said quickly. "Not directly. I haven't... The last night I stayed somewhere with a man... I just..."

"Fuck," Holden breathed. "I thought the guy who killed your roommate was her boyfriend. He was yours?"

"No. He was her boyfriend, but that was the last time... I haven't been with anyone since then. I haven't trusted... I haven't..."

"Jesus, Mack. I'm sorry. I had no idea."

He made a move toward her, then stopped, and Mackenzie felt the loss of him like he'd walked out on her. She wanted him to hold her. To make her feel safe. Even though he was the reason she felt unsafe.

It made no sense, but she felt like she could trust him. That he wasn't the monster she feared every man secretly was deep inside. That Holden was one of the good ones. The kind of man who stood up for others and helped people. Not the kind who killed them while they slept.

Mackenzie wrapped her arms around herself and tried to hold back the tears building inside.

Holden stood across the room, watching her, not moving and not speaking. Just standing there looking like he wasn't sure what the right move was. Then he moved toward the door, away from Mackenzie.

"I'll give you some space." The words were quiet, like it hurt to say them. Then he was gone, into the cold outside the kitchen.

Mackenzie didn't budge from her spot, listening as his footsteps echoed on the metal stairs. He ran down them, getting as far away from her as he could, as quickly as he could.

And then the regret hit. Mackenzie had no right to judge Holden the way so many people had judged her. She was scared of someone who couldn't touch her. Who never touched her. Peter was evil, but he didn't kill Mackenzie. He only killed Jaclyn. Mackenzie never knew why, but she assumed it was so he had someone to blame for Jaclyn's death.

Mackenzie looked around the kitchen, but it was clean. Holden had taken care of everything. It looked as though no one had even been in there.

Without anything else to do, Mackenzie went back to the bunk room. Edie was on her side. Her brown cheeks had a pink flush to them instead of gray. She was still cold, but no longer on the edge of death. Her eyes were closed, but she was there and she was alive.

Noises outside the bunk room drew Mackenzie's attention, but she didn't go out to see what was going on. Holden said he was giving her space, but he probably needed a break from her. From her paranoia and craziness. He shouldn't have followed her. He should have just stayed where he was, and he wouldn't have to worry about her.

The light outside the bunk room faded as the sun set. The overcast skies were still dumping snow on them, but without the sun trying to break through, Mackenzie felt as though nothing outside could reach them.

She stretched out a bunk and tried to read a book. Every so often she heard Holden, but she ignored that and did what she could to get lost in the story she'd been reading.

Until Edie cried out. She shouted something, then groaned and doubled over.

"Holden!" Mackenzie shouted out the door, knowing he'd come.

Mackenzie watched Edie carefully, now silent again, as she laid in the bed.

Holden burst through the door, his gaze wild and fearful. His eyes landed on Mackenzie before he moved toward her. He brushed the hair from her face and studied her. "Are you okay?"

Mackenzie nodded, but Holden continued to look at her.

"Are you hurt? What happened?"

"Edie screamed. She groaned and clutched her stomach, then passed out again."

Holden turned to look at Edie, perfectly still on the bed. He took the few steps to her side and kneeled on the floor next to her. He pressed the back of his hand to her forehead, then pulled it away and rubbed his hands together, blowing into them before he tried again.

"My hands are too cold. I don't know if she has a fever. But it could be starting."

Mackenzie nodded. "I don't know what to do."

"We'll figure it out together." Holden looked at the door, then hung his head. "I tried to dig a path out the front so I could get out of here, so you'd feel safe, but I couldn't get far. I only got a few feet. I don't even know if I was going in the right direction. I'm sorry. But I'll sleep in the ambulance. I won't be able to lock myself inside, but at least I'll be far away from you."

"I don't want that," Mackenzie admitted.

"I want you to feel safe."

"I feel safer with you close."

Holden held her gaze. He didn't look away from her, just stared at her as if waiting for her to tell him she was joking. "A few minutes ago—"

"I'm not afraid of you, Holden. I'm scared, yes, but not of you. I know you'd never hurt me."

"Never."

She smiled and took a tentative step toward him. "Can I... will you..."

"What do you need? Anything?"

"Will you hug me again? Please?" Mackenzie whispered.

Holden stepped closer until they were a breath apart. He waited a painful moment before he closed the last distance between them and pulled her into his arms. Knees to knees, hips to hips, chest to chest. He tucked her head against his shoulder and sighed, as if he needed it as much as she did.

Mackenzie inhaled his scent, a spicy, manly scent combined with a musky smell of a man who'd been working. It stirred something inside her, something long forgotten and buried, and she had the overwhelming desire to feel him moving inside her. His weight above her. His body claiming hers.

Tingles spread across her body and down to her toes. She closed her eyes and let the feeling fill her, letting her body enjoy the idea of desire again.

Holden held her the entire time, not moving away from her even the slightest bit. He grew hard against her belly, but he didn't nudge it against her or make her feel as though she had an obligation to do anything about it.

His hard length made her want him even more. It made her feel like she wasn't the same rejected loser she'd been for years. Someone wanted her. Someone amazing.

Mackenzie leaned back just enough to look up at him. Holden eased his grip on her as if he was letting her go. She lifted on her toes and caught his attention, his face turning toward her seconds before she pressed her lips to his.

He growled. His arms tightened around her body and hauled her impossibly closer. He tilted his head and parted her lips with his tongue, fucking her mouth with his and making every cell in her body stand up and cheer.

Mackenzie whimpered and pressed her fingers to his waist. Firm muscle met her grip. She slid one hand up his back, wanting to touch more of that muscle.

Holden moved one hand to her neck, cupping the back of her head. It rested there for a minute, his thumb rubbing gently on the side of her jaw, a stark contrast to the commanding way he kissed her.

He eased back from the kiss just enough to suck in a deep breath. Mackenzie panted with him, licking her lips to taste him once more.

He tilted her head back and sank into her again, devouring her with another kiss that had her wanting so much more than sanity said she should take. Mackenzie was going to enjoy it. Whatever it was, she was going to get from him.

He pulled back once more and locked his arms around her again, holding her body tight against his. His chest rose and fell with his heavy breaths, hers doing the same.

"I'm trying to be a good guy here, Mackenzie. You make it impossible to hold back."

"What do you mean?"

"I'm manhandling you like I have a right to touch you."

"I kissed you."

"And I'm very happy about that." He breathed a laugh and kissed the side of her head. "But you just told me it's been a long time since you've had anything to do with a man. I'm not going to pressure you into something. Especially when we're trapped in this building with a woman who's going through withdrawal."

"But if we weren't trapped with her you would?" Mackenzie asked, hoping the teasing tone of her voice came through.

Holden chuckled. "No. I wouldn't."

"Good. I said I trust you, Holden. I meant that. It's not something I do easily. Or ever."

"I don't want to break that trust by being a horny shithead."

"You're not. Not even a little."

He leaned back and cupped her jaw, lifting her head until her gaze met his. "I will always back off when you tell me to. I will stop. Whatever. I want you to know that, Mackenzie."

"I know," she whispered, and she did. She fought her attraction to Holden for a long time. She convinced herself she was broken and couldn't figure out who to trust and who not to trust. Peter made her doubt herself so many times after Jaclyn died that Mackenzie never believed in herself after, but she could now. She could trust Holden. He was nothing like Peter. Or anyone else she'd ever known. He was good. Solid. Kind.

Holden kissed her once more on the lips, gently, like he was sealing his promise to her. Then he stepped back and looked at Edie. "I should check on her. If she was calling out, she could be having nightmares."

Mackenzie shivered.

"Are you cold? I tried to block the door downstairs." He kneeled on the floor in front of Edie and pressed his fingers to her neck. He stared at his watch.

"You tried to block the door?"

Holden kept his focus on his watch, then looked up at Mackenzie. "It's only a matter of time before the cold air coming in from outside is stronger than the furnace. I put some fire blankets over the door. I'm not sure it'll work for long, but for now it's better than nothing. We're lucky the door was still intact."

Mackenzie sucked in a breath. She'd almost forgotten about the cold coming in through the collapsed roof. The freezing temperatures invading their little space. The realities outside their walls that they couldn't do anything about.

It was going to be a long night.

8

———

EDIE GROANED IN HER SLEEP AND CLUTCHED HER STOMACH. Holden watched her, feeling hopeless and unable to do anything. He hadn't ever seen a person go through withdrawal before, but he knew it was a horrible experience, one made worse by the quantity of drugs they had been on.

His guess was Edie was going to be miserable for a long time.

"I wonder how she got here," Mackenzie said.

The question had been rolling around in Holden's head since Edie showed up. The roads were shit, but he doubted anyone would have dropped her off anyway. She was kidnapped, held against her will, pumped full of drugs, and God knew what else. It was highly unlikely someone just drove her to the station and left her there.

"She had to have escaped," Mackenzie said. "I wonder how long she was out there alone. And dressed like she was. It's not fair what they did to her."

"No, it isn't," Holden said, even though he got the feeling Mackenzie didn't need him to respond. "But she's safe now. We're not going to let anything happen to her."

"As long as we survive this." Mackenzie looked around the room.

The station was simple. Bunks for them to sleep in when they had long shifts, a kitchen to feed themselves, and places to work. It was fine for a shift, but depending on how long they were stuck there, especially with a gaping hole between them and others, their space might feel far from accommodating.

"Thank you for helping."

"I don't feel like I've done much in the way of helping."

She smiled. "You have. I don't lean on people easily. I have a lot of walls around myself."

"Understandably."

She breathed a laugh. "My therapist says I need to start taking some of those walls down."

"What would she say about us sitting here? Talking about this stuff?"

Mackenzie shook her head and grinned. "She'd think I was making it up."

Holden returned her grin and held her gaze. He wanted to ask her so many things. He wanted to know her. To have her open up to him and tell him all her secrets.

"Why did you and Isabel break up?"

Holden exhaled roughly. "That's what you want to know right now? You could ask me anything and that's the question you ask?"

Mackenzie shrugged. "My last relationship ended because I couldn't get over my best friend being killed and being accused of her murder. My ex-boyfriend didn't stand by me and just faded away. Even when all charges against me were dismissed, he didn't bother calling. Before him, I was too young for any of my relationships to be significant."

"I'm sorry, Mackenzie."

"I am, too." She paused for a long moment, staring at her hands in her lap. She sat on the bunk opposite Edie's, with Holden on one on the other wall, perpendicular to their bunks. "You don't have to tell me about Isabel. I shouldn't have asked."

Holden hadn't told anyone else about his interest in training to be a flight paramedic. After he told Isabel, he worried others would react the same way and stopped thinking about it as much. He knew he had more to offer, but if no one thought he could do it, he wasn't sure he should try.

But the way Mackenzie looked at him made him want to tell her everything about himself. Starting with his secret dream.

"Isabel and I started dating a few years ago. We worked the same shift, and she flirted with me. She was funny and friendly, and I asked her out on a date. She countered by asking me to go out with a group of people from here."

Mackenzie pulled her knees to her chest and leaned against the head of the bed, facing Holden.

"Isabel spent the entire night talking to another guy. I talked to some of our coworkers and realized she wasn't the right person for me. I thought that was the end of it. A few months later, we worked a shift together again, and again she invited me out with this group. One of the guys I'd become friends with was going, so I agreed. This time, Isabel talked to me the whole time."

"You were the center of her attention."

Holden nodded. "I was. I hate to admit it, but I enjoyed it. Everyone else wanted to talk to her, but she focused on me. I felt like I was important."

Mackenzie laughed softly. "I wouldn't expect you to be someone who ever felt like you weren't important."

Holden shrugged. "Everyone has insecurities, I guess. I was never someone praised for anything besides my appearance." His cheeks warmed with the admission. "That sounds vain. I just meant..." Holden drew a breath.

Mackenzie watched him, not hurrying him along, just letting him get his thoughts together.

"My mom was an actress. She was just starting to get big when she had a one-night stand with my dad. He was a delivery driver, and no one special. He was her rebellion, her night of slumming it with the guy on the wrong side of the tracks. She got pregnant, and he insisted on marrying her and taking care of us. She resented him for getting her pregnant, and he hated her for resenting him."

"Wow."

"Yeah. So, anyway, my mom put me in acting and modeling as a kid. Said I had her talent and plopped me in front of a camera as soon as possible. I barely had a childhood because she took me all over to do these jobs. I was told my entire life that I was attractive, but no one ever told me I was smart or kind or anything else. I was good-looking. Nothing more."

"You know that's not true," Mackenzie said.

Holden shrugged.

"Holden, seriously. You're an amazing person. You save people all the time. You've dedicated your life to helping others. You are kind and caring. You have to be smart to know what to do in these situations. I mean, look at right now? Most people would not think twice about calling the cops and letting someone else deal with Edie, but you're here with me. You made dinner for us and sealed the door so we don't freeze to death. You even tried to leave me here because you knew I was scared. You've been nothing but amazing. Why would you ever think you are only good-looking and nothing more?"

"Thank you," Holden whispered. His throat was tight and tingly. Her words meant more than she could possibly know. And they gave him the courage to tell her the rest.

"I'm serious," Mackenzie said. She got up from her bunk and moved to his. She took his hand and held it between hers. "You're an amazing man."

Holden squeezed her hand. "Thank you. That means a lot."

"It's the truth."

He smiled and continued with his story. "Things with Isabel were good for a while. We would get together when we could, go out when we were both off. I liked her, but there was always something that held me back from getting too serious with her. I told myself it was because I wasn't ready to settle down yet, but she never pushed for that. We were having fun."

Mackenzie rubbed her thumb along the back of Holden's hand, silently encouraging him.

"We were off and on for a long time. A few years. The last time we got together was a few months ago. I thought maybe we would figure things out. I'd decided I was done with the back and forth and that if things didn't work out, I was done for good."

"And things obviously didn't work out."

Holden shook his head. "I was talking to her about my career. About what I want to do. And she laughed at me."

Mackenzie tilted her head and narrowed her eyes. "What did you tell her you want to do?"

Holden swallowed and met her gaze. "I want to train to be a flight paramedic."

Mackenzie's brows shot up. A smile slowly lifted her lips. "You would be amazing at that."

"You don't have to say that." Holden pulled his hand from hers.

"I'm not. I mean it. You are very calm under pressure. I've seen that today. Major things don't seem to faze you. You're strong, which sounds like a vanity thing, but sometimes holding on inside there can be tricky. And most importantly, it's what you want. That's a big job. It's a tough job. It's different from what you do now, but similar enough that you have an idea of what it would take. That means you have to want to do it."

"Isabel told me I don't need to do something like that. That more training..."

"What did she say?" Mackenzie whispered, her voice dangerous.

"She said people like her and me don't need to do more training. We just need to smile and we get our way."

Mackenzie breathed a laugh and shook her head. She jumped off the bunk and paced, arms flailing as she spoke. "I figured she was like that. You know, Jaclyn's boyfriend was like that. He thought he was untouchable. That's why he accused me of killing her. Because I'm nobody. I'm invisible. I'm unclaimed and unwanted and—"

"You're not unwanted," Holden said softly.

"Oh, please. I know what I am. I have this job because people can't see me. They don't judge me based on my appearance. I'm the exact opposite of Isabel. I'm frumpy and curvy and undesirable. I keep to myself and don't let others in. I don't flirt with anyone and I'd get laughed at if I did. No man has ever spent months hoping for a tiny bit of attention from me."

"I have."

Mackenzie gasped at his admission and spun toward him. Her rant had her eyes blazing and her cheeks pink with frustration.

She was stunning. Staring at her, seeing the passion in her gaze and the strength in who she was, made Holden want her that much more.

And she didn't laugh at him. She didn't tell him he was ridiculous for wanting to become a flight paramedic. She didn't make him feel like he was nothing more than a pretty face.

"What?" Mackenzie gasped after a full minute. "No. That's not true."

Holden scooted off the bed and stood before her. He kept his hands to himself, but he ached to put them on her. To cup her jaw and tilt it up until she surrendered to him and let him devour her.

"Holden."

"I have an entire kitchen here. Why do you think I come to your side of the building for snacks? We have bunk rooms and bathrooms and everything we could possibly need. But I find excuses to see you. To run into you and talk to you. Pour you a cup of coffee and pretend you agreed to it instead of me standing around until you show up."

"Holden."

"I like you, Mackenzie. You're smart, and you're strong. You are so caring. You hide your emotions well, but the first time I saw you get upset because of a call, I wanted to pull you into my arms and never let you go."

"When was that?" she whispered.

"Eight months ago. And every time since."

"Eight months?" She looked up at him with wide eyes behind her glasses. Innocent and honest. Kind.

"Yeah. I know I'm probably not doing anything more

than scaring you off, but yeah. You're not like Isabel. You don't flaunt your body and get people to do things for you because you're gorgeous. You—"

"Because I'm not," she said.

Holden couldn't stop himself from cupping her jaw at her words. "Oh, Mackenzie, you have no idea. You make me crazy. When you walk away from me, these curvy hips shifting from side to side, it's all I can do to keep from crawling out of my skin. You don't see yourself the same way I do, and that's okay, but you are definitely gorgeous."

"I... Thank you."

Holden smiled at her and leaned closer. "Can I kiss you, Mackenzie?"

Mackenzie tilted her chin up and nodded, just once.

IT WASN'T A KISS. Not even close. It was a seduction. A teaser. A preamble to all the ways he was going to make her crazy.

And he was starting now.

Good Lord, the man could kiss. The other two times, when she threw herself at him, didn't disappoint, but this time, when he was the one in control, when he started it, her toes curled in an instant.

Mackenzie inhaled, drawing him closer with her breath. He surrounded her, every part of her body feeling like it was catered to by him. His hands drifted from her jaw over her throat. One went down her back and pressed against her spine, bringing her body into full contact with his. His other hand slid into her hair, tilting her head to give him better access to devour her mouth until she whimpered.

He pulled back just enough to dive in again, tilting her head with a tug on her hair and taking a step toward her that had her backing up. Her leg hit the edge of the bunk they'd been sitting on, and Holden turned them. He broke their kiss long enough to sit on the bed, pulling her down with him.

She straddled him, his hard length thick between them. Her body jolted at the contact, seeking relief she hadn't realized she needed until his erection rubbed against her clit.

"Mackenzie," he groaned. He yanked her body against his, the friction he created making her gasp again.

Mackenzie ran her hands through his hair and let herself get lost, just for a minute. She hadn't let go once in almost a decade. She'd held herself back from pleasure and joy, from excitement and desire, from all the things Holden was promising with his body. She wanted to give in, to have all those things again, but she wasn't sure she could do it.

"You're in charge here, Mack," Holden whispered against her skin. His lips trailed from her ear to her collarbone and back to her lips. He pulled back just enough to meet her gaze. "Nothing is going to happen unless you want it to."

"I..."

"There's no pressure. I want you, Mackenzie. You can feel that. But I'm not going anywhere."

She sucked in a breath and nodded, leaning down to capture his lips again. Her hips moved with their kiss, rubbing her clit against the ridge in his pants.

His fingers tightened on her hips, urging her to keep going. One fingertip slipped beneath her shirt, bare skin on bare skin, and Mackenzie nearly lost her mind.

"Please," she gasped.

"Anything."

"Touch me," she whispered.

Holden didn't wait for her to ask him a second time, he just went for it. He eased her shirt up and splayed his hand wide across her belly. He lifted both hands, drawing her shirt up and off.

Mackenzie reached behind herself for her bra, unhooking it and dropping it on the bed next to her knee.

Holden stared at her for so long she thought he'd changed his mind. She moved to cover herself, but he growled at her. "I'm enjoying the view." He trailed one fingertip lightly over her skin, lifting goosebumps where he touched her. She shivered, feeling like a goddess.

He lifted one breast to his lips. He met her gaze as he reached out for the peak with his tongue.

She sucked in a breath when he licked her nipple. It was simple, barely even erotic, but it was more than she'd experienced in years. It was contact, and it was trust, and it was hot as fuck.

Holden licked and sucked her nipple until Mackenzie's hips shifted again. Then he moved to the other one and teased her some more. She sighed and panted and begged without words for him to keep touching her.

"Where else do you want me to touch you?" he whispered.

"Make me come. Please," she gasped as he bit down on her nipple.

Again, he didn't hesitate. He eased his hand into the front of her yoga pants, the fabric stretching easily to give him space. His palm rested flat against her belly, his fingers easing slowly toward her entrance.

They both groaned when he pressed one finger deep into her. "Fucking hell, Mack. You're so fucking wet."

"It's been a while," she said, feeling embarrassed.

"It means a lot to have you trust me," he said, erasing her shame and fear.

"Oh, God," she gasped as he added a second finger, stretching her tight channel.

"How do you like to come? Inside or on your clit?"

"Both," she confessed. She'd never told anyone that before. No one had ever asked.

For a brief second, she wondered if she should be sharing so much with Holden. Was he going to run back and tell the others he'd fucked the killer? Was he using her to make Isabel jealous? Was he serious about wanting her?

Then he pressed his thumb to her clit and Mackenzie stopped thinking entirely. She was liquid desire, her body not caring about anything besides riding the wave that was building far too quickly inside her.

Holden was good with his hands. Damn good. His fingers slid deep into her, slamming hard and spiraling her body up and up and up. And his thumb swiped all her wetness over her clit, the delicious wet friction making her gasp for every breath until she was sure she would pass out.

And then he kissed her. His lips on her nipples, then his tongue across her exposed breasts. Then he kissed his way up until he captured her lips.

Mackenzie stopped fighting. She stopped thinking. She stopped wondering *why me?* and enjoyed the wild ride Holden was taking her on because once the storm was gone and the rest of the world invaded their tiny little world, she'd lose him to Isabel and flight paramedic training and work and all the beautiful people who had a claim on one of their own.

Holden's tongue plunged into her mouth the same instant her body released. She threw her head back and cried out, the force of her orgasm shocking her. Her hips rocked over his hand and her breasts bounced wildly in his face. All her rolls and folds quivered and wobbled, and all

Holden did was push her forward into another orgasm that was just as powerful as the first and even more of a surprise.

Mackenzie had never come twice in one night before. Her vision went black around the edges, and her breath stalled in her lungs. She felt like she was flying, floating, free. Nothing could touch her.

"You're so beautiful," Holden whispered against her neck.

"That was..."

"I agree," he said. His eyes crinkled on the edges when he smiled. He cupped the back of her head with one hand and pulled her down for a kiss that was both sweet and demanding as he withdrew his hand from between her thighs. "I'll be right back."

She tilted her head in question but climbed off him so he could get up. His erection led the way to the attached bathroom. Water ran, and a minute later, he was back.

"Are you... I mean, do you..."

"We should sleep while Edie's sleeping. Any chance I can talk you into sharing this bunk with me?"

"But you didn't come," Mackenzie blurted.

"I didn't start kissing you for any reason than because I wanted to kiss you. I'd love to sink into you right now and let my eyes roll back in my head, but I don't have a condom, and I'm not the kind of guy who's going to have a woman on her knees before I can even take her on a date."

"Oh."

"I told you I like you, Mackenzie. I meant it. And watching you lose your mind tonight was amazing. I'm hoping I get to see that again, and that maybe I get to join you, but I also want you to know you can trust me, and until we're there, I'm good."

"I do trust you."

"I hope so. Get some sleep tonight. Shirt optional as far as I'm concerned." He grinned salaciously and winked at her.

Mackenzie didn't know that side of Holden, but she liked it. She felt almost normal. And she was definitely tired.

She moved her shirt and bra to the bunk she'd abandoned and curled up on the bed that was almost too small for her alone, and more than laughable with the two of them together. Holden laid on his back and stretched his arm out, letting her snuggle up next to him. He pulled the blankets up around them and drew a deep breath.

"Thank you, Mackenzie. For sharing yourself with me."

"Thank you."

He kissed the top of her head. "Get some sleep."

"You, too."

9

———

Holden wanted to lie in that bed and hold Mackenzie forever. He couldn't remember the last time he'd been so satisfied without doing more than touching a woman. But no other woman had ever been like Mackenzie.

Edie stirred in her sleep and groaned again. She'd been doing that more and more as Mackenzie slept. Holden knew there was nothing he could do for Edie, but he hated that she was in so much pain. He hated that she'd gone through a hell he couldn't even imagine someone being put through. He would do anything to keep her safe and help her heal. No one deserved what she'd been through.

Holden drifted in and out of sleep while Mackenzie snored softly on his chest. A cry that was far more than a groan woke him and had him looking across the room toward Edie.

She was doubled over again, but her brow was beaded with sweat and her face twisted in pain. Holden eased himself from under a sleeping Mackenzie, already missing the warmth of her half-naked body against his, and hurried to the bathroom.

Holden ran a hand towel under the faucet and carried the damp cloth back to Edie. After cutting her clothes off, he hadn't looked for anything else, and the way she was burning up told him that might not have been the best move.

He pressed the towel to her forehead. She winced and pulled away, but didn't open her eyes. When he did it again, she whimpered but let him wipe down her overheated skin. After a few minutes, she settled and slept soundly once more, her groans fading. He tucked the blankets around her again and carried the towel back to the bathroom. He rinsed it and hung it on the towel rack to dry in case he needed it again.

Holden tried to sneak back into the room, but the door squeaked and Mackenzie jerked upright. The blanket fell to her waist, her breasts bare to his gaze. He hardened instantly.

"What happened?" Mackenzie blurted.

"Edie was making noise. I wiped her face with a towel. She settled again."

"Oh." Mackenzie looked toward the sleeping woman. "I still can't believe she's here. That she's alive."

Holden nodded. "Yeah. I mean, I didn't really know the whole story, but it sounds crazy. I wonder what happened to her."

Mackenzie shuddered and pulled the blanket up to her shoulders. "I don't know. But the man who did this to her is going to pay."

"Damon something, right? It was on the news."

Mackenzie nodded. "Damon Street. He's evil. The things he's done."

"You know about him?" Holden asked.

Mackenzie met his gaze in the darkness. She didn't move

for a long moment, and when she did, she nodded once. "I've been doing some research. His name has come up in more than one call. He's been killing people for years. Right under the noses of the police."

"That's why you said we couldn't call them. Because someone has to be working with him."

She nodded again. "I'm still trying to figure the whole thing out, but yeah. And when he's done, he'll kill them and move on."

Holden sucked in a breath. "All the calls we take, the people we go out to find, we try to help people. To save people when all hope is almost lost. To know there's someone out there intentionally working to offset all the work we do feels... hopeless."

"No. We can't be hopeless. We have to keep fighting. Men like Damon Street win when we give up. They win when we stop doing everything in our power to erase their bad with our good."

Holden looked at Mackenzie for a long moment. Long enough that she squirmed and asked, "What?"

Holden shook his head. "You're pretty amazing. Everything you've been through, I think a lot of people would have stopped believing in good, stopped trying. But you just keep going after it. Keep fighting."

"I have to. We all have to. If not, more women like Edie will vanish. Even more women who aren't like Edie. She had a cousin. She had someone who came looking for her. Tonya paid for it, but Edie wasn't one of the forgotten. I can't even guess how many Damon killed over the years that were. Unclaimed, forgotten, unknown. Forever."

Mackenzie shivered and wrapped her arms tighter around herself.

Holden sat next to her on the bed and leaned against the

wall. His gaze flickered between the two women he was trapped with and felt guilty for being grateful he was there instead of on the other side in the call center.

"No one deserves that," Holden whispered.

Mackenzie shook her head, then wiped her cheek.

He looked at her, her eyes shining in the darkness with unshed tears. Another one raced down her cheeks before she wiped it away. "I'm one of the unclaimed."

"Why would you say that?"

"Because it's true." Her whispered voice broke. She drew a breath and let it out slowly. "Jaclyn was my only family. My mom died when I was young. My dad remarried and made a life with my step-mom and her sons. I don't really talk to them, and if something ever happened to me, they'd never know. I don't have other family or friends. It was just me and Jaclyn in college. We were going to get an apartment together when we graduated and build a life together. She was like the sister I never had, and I was the same for her. No guy ever came between us. No one did. Until Peter took her from me forever."

"I'm sorry." Holden knew the words weren't enough, and they weren't what he wanted to say to her. He wanted to tell her he'd notice if something ever happened to her. He'd come looking. He'd be her family. But he knew it was too soon for all of that, so he just reached for her hand and held it in the silence of the night.

MACKENZIE DIDN'T LIKE BEING vulnerable. She didn't like opening herself up to others. But there was something about Holden that had her confessing all the things she'd never admitted to anyone else. She tried to tell herself it was being trapped together or it was taking care of Edie together or it was just the darkness of night and being tired, but she knew none of those things were the truth. The truth was, she liked Holden. She trusted him. And that scared the hell out of her.

Holden's hand was warm and comforting on hers. After a minute, she shifted to lean against his side, taking strength from him that she'd never leaned on another person for. Mackenzie had done a lot of things on her own, including turning over abusive husbands and boyfriends to police and convincing the women they hurt to testify against them. She wasn't scared of death or retaliation or exposure. She didn't care if anything happened to her. She only cared about the women she'd helped over the years.

But as she sat there with her hand in Holden's and her head on his shoulder, watching Edie sleep, she knew all those men she helped to put away didn't begin to compare to Damon Street. He was an evil Mackenzie only thought she'd faced before. Seeing his handiwork, listening to Penny die and watching Edie suffer, Damon was worse than all the other men she'd faced combined.

"The first time I got a call from a woman who was being abused by her husband, I talked to her until the police arrived. She'd locked herself in the bathroom. They took her to the hospital, but he showed up and apologized and she went back to him. A few months later, she called again, and I answered. She found out she was pregnant, and he went crazy and beat her until she miscarried. She left him, but the damage was done."

Holden squeezed her hand and flipped his to wrap his fingers through hers.

"The next time I got a call like that, I told her not to go back to him afterward, no matter what. She ended up hanging up on me before the police arrived. I never heard from her again. The third one I got was a woman who'd left her boyfriend. He hit her and she ran, and she called when she was outside because she was barefoot and hurting. She testified against him and ended up leaving the area, moving back to where her family was."

"How many calls do you get like that?" Holden whispered.

"Two or three a month, usually."

"Jesus."

"I've learned how to tell which ones are likely to go back and which ones will fight. I've listened to women die after the third or fourth call when they kept going back, even though I tried to help them. And I've been a witness to trials where men have tried to sue their wife or girlfriend for assault after she fought back."

"Holy shit."

"I don't know what happened to Edie or how she got here, but I know she's been through a kind of hell I've never even heard of before. She's been assaulted and drugged and likely raped and beaten. She's lucky to be alive, but I know not all women feel that way. She might wish she'd died in that storm."

"It won't be easy for her, but she's a fighter. She pounded on that door because she wanted to live. She wasn't out there to give up."

Mackenzie nodded. "I hope you're right."

They were both silent for a long time, watching Edie sleep restlessly across the room. Mackenzie was tired, but fear and anger burned in her gut. How many others were there? How many more women had Damon Street taken? How many had he killed?

Holden's warmth made Mackenzie's eyes droop. Before

long, she was yawning and drifting back to sleep on Holden's shoulder, still naked from the waist up.

A scream woke Mackenzie a while later. She sat up quickly, blinking the sleep from her eyes as she tried to figure out where she was and what was going on.

"I'm here to help you," Holden whispered.

"I won't take any more of your drugs. I don't want it," Edie sobbed.

"Edie. You're safe," Mackenzie said. She wrapped the blanket around her shoulders and pulled it tight to cover herself, then moved to Edie's bed. She sat on the edge and regarded the other woman. "You're in a rescue station."

Edie looked around. The morning light was filtering through the high windows around the darkening shades. Edie's eyes were wide with fear and unease. She clutched the blanket to her chest.

"Why am I almost naked? Why are we both? If he's here to help us, why would he have taken our clothes off? We're not safe here," Edie whimpered.

Mackenzie grabbed her shirt and turned her back, pulling it on over her head. Her cheeks burned. She never thought about how it would look when Edie woke up. She hated that she brought more fear to the woman.

"You showed up at the door during the snowstorm. We let you in and you were freezing, hypothermic. We had to cut your clothes off because they were soaked through," Holden explained calmly. He stood a few feet away, giving Edie space but also blocking her escape.

"And you didn't bother to find me more clothes?" Edie snapped.

"We were trying to be respectful."

Edie raised a brow. "Then why wasn't she wearing a shirt? Was that being respectful, too?"

Mackenzie couldn't look at Holden. Her entire face flamed. She shifted on the bed and Edie looked at her. "That was different."

Edie narrowed her eyes until realization dawned. "Are you kidding me? I'm in the middle of a fucking porno or some shit. What the fuck?"

"It wasn't like that," Mackenzie said. "We... I'm sorry. We shouldn't have done anything. We should have been more considerate of you."

"You think?" Edie looked around. "Who else is here?"

"It's just the three of us," Mackenzie said.

"That's not possible. This place is always crawling with people." Edie started to climb out of bed, but stopped and glared at Holden. "A little privacy?"

Holden nodded and walked out the door into the cold hallway.

"Can I ask you a question?" Mackenzie asked.

Edie raised a brow.

"Are you Edie Warren?"

"How do you know my name?"

Mackenzie sucked in a breath and nearly cried. "You've been missing for months. Your cousin, Tonya, was looking for you."

"You know Tonya? Where is she? Is she here?"

Mackenzie's heart squeezed. There was a tiny piece of her that had hoped she wasn't Edie Warren because Mackenzie didn't want to have the conversation they had to have. That tiny piece felt like a betrayal. Mackenzie wanted Edie to be safe, but she hated that she was going to take away the last hope Edie had.

"Tonya came here looking for you. She hired a private investigator who found a woman he believed was connected to the man responsible for your disappearance. When Tonya went to speak to the woman, she was killed."

"Tonya's dead?" Edie gasped. "No. It's not possible. You're lying!"

Holden burst through the door, his gaze flickering between the two women. "Mackenzie?"

"It's fine, Holden."

Edie raced toward Holden, swinging her fists at him. "You're wrong. Tonya's not dead. Let me out of here. I need to find her."

Holden caught Edie around the waist and carried her back to the bed. Just as quickly as she fought him, she went limp in his arms. Holden laid her on the bed and pulled the blanket around her.

Edie sobbed, all her energy drained from the small outburst. "Tonya," she whimpered into her pillow as the fight faded from her and she fell asleep again.

Mackenzie rolled her lips in and sank her teeth into the bottom one. It wasn't fair. None of it was fair. She hated Damon for taking Edie, for putting her through whatever she'd been through, and for killing Tonya.

"I'm sorry," Holden said quietly.

Mackenzie shook her head. She couldn't speak. She didn't blame him, but she knew if she spoke, she wouldn't be able to hold back her emotions. After all she'd shared with Holden in the last twenty-four hours, the anger and pain inside her was too raw.

He moved toward her, something she felt more than heard. His arms came around her, pulling her into his body.

Mackenzie fought him for a minute, not wanting to let the pain out. She needed to hold on to it, to keep it inside. She couldn't let Holden see her weakness. And she couldn't deal with it. If she processed the pain and let go of it, she wouldn't have the strength to do what she knew she needed to do. She wouldn't be able to take down Damon Street.

HOLDEN HELD Mackenzie until her body softened and the first sob broke free. He didn't know what her connection was to Edie or Tonya, but there was clearly one there. More than she'd let on.

Her weight dropped, like she couldn't support herself, and Holden tightened his grip on her. He wasn't going to let her fall. He shifted them to the bed they'd slept on and sat down, pulling her onto his lap. She curled into him, sobbing and choking and whimpering. It tore a hole inside Holden to hear a woman as strong as Mackenzie fall apart like she was. He didn't know Edie's whole story, and he clearly didn't know as much as Mackenzie, but her reaction said it was far worse than he imagined it could possibly be.

Mackenzie cried, and Edie slept. Holden watched them both, feeling like a loyal canine keeping guard over his people. When Mackenzie cried herself to sleep, Holden kept holding her, wishing he could do something to ease the pain she felt.

Something solid dug into his side, and he realized it was Mackenzie's phone. He didn't want to violate her privacy, but surely using her phone to research Damon Street was okay. Right?

He tapped the screen to wake it up and held it in front of Mackenzie to unlock it. He found the browser at the bottom and clicked on it. A search page came up. Holden hesitated for a minute, unsure if he should look up Damon or Edie. He typed in Edie's name and waited.

Not many posts appeared. There were a few that

mentioned Edie and her cousin, Tonya, but it wasn't long before the posts had nothing to do with her. Holden read what he could find, including a report on the press conference from the week before.

He searched Tonya Warren next. There was a bit more about her, including the name of the private investigator she'd hired to find her cousin. Holden looked into him and found a connection to Karli Sloane, the woman Tonya was mistaken for.

Holden kept digging, reading more and more about the twisted tale that led Edie to where she was on the cot across the room from him. He finally got it. He finally started to understand why Mackenzie was so protective of a woman she'd never met before. By the time either woman stirred, Holden felt the same fierce protective instinct. About both of them.

He was going to make sure nothing happened to either woman ever again.

10

———

Mackenzie spent the next day watching the windows for any sign of life outside. She checked in with the call center twice, but there was nothing she could do to help, and nothing they could do to get to her.

Edie slept most of the day. She woke up a few times and drank some water, ate a few crackers, and begged for drugs. She propositioned both Holden and Mackenzie if they would share the good stuff with her. It broke Mackenzie's heart to hear.

Late in the day, Mackenzie checked in with Captain Patrick to see if there was any chance they would be rescued.

"The storm dropped more snow than we expected. Until we can get some big trucks in and remove it, we're mostly trapped."

"The entire city?" Mackenzie screeched. She'd never heard if it being that bad. They were equipped and prepared. They should have been fine.

"Unfortunately, yeah." Marcus sighed heavily. "The city wasn't as prepared as they thought they were. People are trapped all over. I know your situation isn't ideal, but you're safe. Safer than some. And she's safe. That's enough to give me some hope right now."

Mackenzie drew a ragged breath. "You're right. I know you are. It's just hard to believe it's so bad."

"It is. I'm still trying to figure out how Edie made it to you."

"I am, too. She hasn't been awake long enough to ask her. The one time she was, we told her about Tonya."

"I'm sorry you had to do that."

Mackenzie sniffed at the memory. "She needed to know. We will find Damon and make sure he pays for what he's done to them."

"I agree. And as soon as we can get to you, we will. I already have a safe place for Edie to go into rehab under an assumed name. It's set up. When she feels well enough to be released, we'll make sure she's safe."

"He's never going to touch her again." Mackenzie burned with rage.

"No. He's not. Stay safe."

"You, too."

Mackenzie hung up and turned her phone off to save the battery. Then she went to find Holden.

He was back in the kitchen, stirring something on the stove. It smelled good and made her stomach rumble. "Hungry?"

She chuckled. "I seem to always be hungry. There's nothing else to do here. I'm used to working and then... Going home." Mackenzie didn't want to tell him what she normally did in her downtime.

"What were you really going to say?"

"Nothing." The answer was too quick, but Holden didn't push. Mackenzie wasn't sure he'd really want her to answer.

To tell him that she'd made it her business to track down the men who abused their wives and girlfriends and make sure they stopped. She'd threatened more than a few and made some enemies, but she'd never crossed a line. She'd never hurt anyone, just made a few threats.

"I'm used to going out on calls. I'm feeling unsettled just sitting around."

"I'm sorry you got trapped here with me."

"I'm not," he said without hesitation. "I might not love being trapped, but I'm very happy it's with you."

Mackenzie smiled, hoping he still felt that way after they were free and he could go back to his life.

"Have you checked on Edie?"

Mackenzie shook her head. "I was talking to Captain Patrick."

"I heard. You two sound close."

"Nope. I'm still not entirely sure he trusts me. We've only met twice."

"Twice?"

Mackenzie nodded. "The first time was when I was trying to prove Jessica German killed Karli Sloane and I let myself into the house where she was staying. Captain Patrick was there with a bunch of others, planning out the press conference."

"Are you serious?"

"Yeah. I... It was just like Jaclyn. She called second, like Peter did. She said she found the body, like Peter did. I just..."

Holden crossed the room and pulled her into his arms. She breathed his musky scent and rested her head on his chest. She liked leaning on him, letting him carry some of her burden. It was dangerous, but she couldn't find the strength to resist.

"I'm so fucking sorry you went through that."

"Thanks."

"Do you still think Jessica German did it?"

Mackenzie shrugged and stepped out of his embrace. She ran her hands down her arms to erase the chill she felt being out of his arms. "I don't know. I think a part of me wonders, but I know they caught the guy who actually did it. And hearing how many cases are tied back to Damon Street makes me think it's very possible this is all connected."

"How many cases? What do you mean?"

Mackenzie hadn't meant to admit that. "Oh, you know, Jessica and Karli, and Edie, and um…"

"Your research? I thought you were just looking at old calls."

Mackenzie hugged her middle and straightened her spine. She was not going to let him tell her she couldn't do it. That she should let the police handle it or something. She knew how the police worked. She knew they weren't always looking for the person who was actually guilty, just someone they could convict. Justice didn't always get served. Sometimes people needed to help it along.

"Mackenzie, he's dangerous. If he knows about you—"

"I don't care," she said, her voice full of steel.

"How can you not care?"

She breathed a mirthless laugh. "I already told you, I'm one of the unclaimed, unwanted. If someone like him kills me, but it stops him from hurting others, it'll be worth it."

"You can't possibly mean that."

"I do. More than you know."

"What does that mean?"

"It means I'm not going to sit back and let the men handle shit. I'm going to fight. I'm going to go down swinging. Hard. And I intend to do some damage in the process."

"Mack, what did you do?"

The horrified look on his face was enough to temper her anger. Not enough for her to stop feeling so angry. Damon Street was not a man who deserved protection. He was evil. He killed people for pleasure. He tortured people and drugged them and traded them to others for God only knew what purpose. He wasn't someone who should be above ground when so many others were six feet under thanks to him.

"Mackenzie, talk to me."

She grunted and glared at him. "I didn't do anything to Damon Street. But if I ever had the chance, I'd kill him."

"You can't say things like that."

"Why? It's true. Why wouldn't I? You see what he did to Edie. She's only one of dozens, hundreds, thousands maybe. He's been doing this for decades. Killing people, drugging people, raping people. And that's just the direct contact. What about the drugs and guns he's put on the streets? He has no concern for others. He's only out for himself. And he's built an organization of people who think like him and act like him and they're all doing the same thing. It can't continue."

"I agree, but you can't kill him."

"I'm not out there looking for him. But if I find him, I won't think twice about it."

"Mack—"

"No, Holden. Don't try to tell me it's wrong. I can't accept that. I'm willing to go to jail to put him in the dirt. I don't care. He doesn't deserve to breathe."

"Oh, Mackenzie," Holden whispered. He reached for her. He wiped a tear from her cheek, then gently pulled her into his embrace.

She didn't realize she was crying until he wiped her tear,

but once she was safely in his arms, the dam broke. She cried until she sobbed, then she cried some more. She couldn't stop herself once she started thinking about all the women Damon had hurt over the years. All the women his people had hurt. All the deaths and victims, all the drugs and violence. All because one man decided to make himself a god.

"Please promise me you won't go looking for him alone. If you ever think you found him, tell me and I'll go with you."

"I..." Mackenzie thought about it. Could she stick to that promise if she made it? Would she call him? Or would she go alone like she'd always done? All the men who beat their wives who never knew she was the one who left notes for them. Who left knives in their tires. Who increased the threats to them until they finally left town and left their women alone.

She didn't get all of them. Some of the men retaliated first. Some of them couldn't be scared. Some were vicious and cruel. But she saved more than would have been saved if she'd done nothing. If she'd sat on the sidelines and waited for someone else to help.

"I'm not sure I can promise that," she admitted.

Holden closed his eyes and sucked in a breath. "I don't think I can handle it if something happens to you."

"We barely know each other. How can you say that?"

"Because I care about you. You might say we barely know each other, but I don't feel that way. I feel like I know you, Mack. And I don't want to lose you, even if it means Damon Street is above ground."

Mackenzie seethed at the idea, but she tried to let in the concern. Holden wasn't choosing Damon's life over hers. He wanted her alive, and for Damon to get the justice he deserved.

"I'll try."

He squeezed her to him and kissed the top of her head. "I'll take it."

ANOTHER NIGHT WENT by and they were still trapped. Holden was ready to dig their way out with his bare hands. Not because he wanted to get away from Mackenzie, or Edie, but because he knew he was at the edge of his capabilities with Edie. If she didn't start to improve soon, he was afraid she wouldn't. If she was in a medical facility, they would have given her more fluids and meds to manage the symptoms she was experiencing.

And counseling. She was going to need lots of it. Not just for the addiction that had been forced on her, but for everything else. Her own trauma and losing her cousin.

Holden eased out of bed, leaving a sleeping Mackenzie curled up against the wall. He wasn't sleeping much sharing a twin bed, but it was better than having her out of reach. She tried after their first night on the tiny bed together, but he joined her and gave her no option.

The hallway was still freezing, but Holden braved it anyway. He needed to check on the fire blankets he put up around the door to make sure it was still holding somewhat. The crisp air was better than coffee to wake him up.

Once he assured himself it was as good as it could be, he went back upstairs. Both women were still sleeping, so Holden headed to the weight room. He lifted weights, then got on the treadmill and ran a quick two miles. When he was done, he checked on Mackenzie and Edie once more, then started the coffee and jumped in the shower.

The hot water felt good on his body. Even though they hadn't lost power yet, the cold was seeping in more and more every day. If they didn't get out of there soon, they were going to have to do something different to stay warm.

When Holden got out of the shower, he dried himself off and changed into the last clean outfit he had. He was thankful he'd planned ahead and packed for a few days when he came into work before the storm. He finally gave up on being considerate and had been pilfering through his coworkers things to find clothes for Mackenzie and Edie to wear, but they were all running low on options.

It was definitely time for a rescue.

Mackenzie was sitting at the counter and sipping from a mug when Holden walked into the kitchen. She was wrapped in a blanket and still deliciously mussed from sleep, her eyes barely open behind her glasses.

"Morning," he said.

She grunted in response.

Holden grinned. He wasn't exactly a morning person, but he wasn't opposed to them. Especially when they were shared with Mackenzie. "What do you want for breakfast?"

"Coffee."

He chuckled. "Pancakes it is."

She grunted once more but didn't argue.

Holden got out the supplies and mixed the batter from memory. He added the chocolate chips he found the night before and set a plate in front of Mackenzie as she sat down with her second cup.

"What's in it?"

"Chocolate chips. I figured chocolate is always a good idea."

"Unless you're allergic."

"Shit. You are? I didn't know. Don't eat that."

"I'm not, but chocolate wouldn't be a good idea if I was."

Holden gasped for breath, the panic slowly dissipating inside him. "You're not allergic?"

She shook her head and shoved a bite into her mouth.

"You scared the hell out of me."

She shrugged and speared another bite, holding it up as she chewed.

Holden chuckled and went back to making pancakes. When he was done, he joined her for a cup of coffee and a few pancakes.

"How did you sleep?" he asked after a minute.

"Not long enough."

"I'm with you."

"You were up forever ago."

"Wanted to make sure everything is okay."

"Do you think we're going to get out of here anytime soon?"

"I hope so. It's nice and sunny outside. I thought I heard some vehicles when I was downstairs earlier. Maybe that'll mean they can get the roads cleared."

"I'm going to check in with Captain Patrick. See if he has any updates."

Holden nodded as Mackenzie dragged her feet to the bunk room in search of her phone. He put a pancake on a plate and cleaned up the rest of the kitchen, then followed Mackenzie.

Edie was still sleeping. Mackenzie wasn't in the bunk room, but her voice said she was close. Holden set the plate down on the table next to Edie's bed and opened the door to see if Mackenzie was in the hallway.

"That's great news. Thank you. See you soon."

Mackenzie hung up and looked up at Holden with a smile. "They're on the way here now."

"Really?"

Mackenzie nodded. "Crews have been working to clear roads and Marcus pushed for them to clear the road here. Out front is still a mess, but they're going to get someone to plow us out and they're going to take Edie to rehab before anyone knows she's here."

"Shit. We're almost free."

"Almost." Mackenzie's smile faded as she said the word.

Holden wondered if she was thinking the same thing he was. Their bubble was about to burst. They'd been holed up together and sharing a bed, food, and body heat for days. They'd been taking care of Edie and trying to figure out her story. And now, they were about to go back to the lives they led before. Separate.

"Let's go see if we can get Edie up." Mackenzie avoided Holden's gaze and ducked around him to go into the bunk room. She was sitting on the side of Edie's bed when Holden walked in a minute later.

"Someone's coming?" Edie asked, her voice small and scared.

"He's the police captain. We can trust him. I promise you."

"Is he going to take me back to them?"

"No," Mackenzie said firmly. "He's going to take you to rehab first. He already has a spot for you. Under a different name. No one is going to know you're there."

"Not even you?" Edie asked.

Mackenzie faltered, her lip quivering before she bit down on it. She forced a smile as her eyes filled with unshed tears. "I don't know. But I'd like to see you if that's allowed."

Edie nodded, tears rolling down her cheeks. The two

women leaned toward each other and hugged. They cried and laughed and whispered things Holden couldn't hear, and when they pulled apart, they held hands.

"I'm so sorry about Tonya," Mackenzie said.

Edie sucked in a breath. "Thank you. I hate that someone hurt her. That she died because of me."

"No. You had nothing to do with it. The man who killed her, and the one who ordered him to do it, are the ones to blame. Not you. Never you."

Edie smiled and nodded. "Thank you."

"Can I ask you a question?" Mackenzie said.

Edie nodded.

"How did you get here? I mean, people have been looking for you and you just showed up. During a blizzard."

Edie shrugged. "I'm not entirely sure. I was mostly kept at one house. The guy there..." She shivered. "Someone came and grabbed me. I think he looked familiar, and I was so high I barely knew what was going on. He had me sneak out a window, and he drove me somewhere else. He put me in a room and left, locked the door. He was going to kill me. I'm not sure how I knew with all the drugs in my system, but I knew. I found a window. I unlocked it and got out. I must have walked here, but I don't really remember. I knew it was my only chance to live, though. The only one I was going to get. If I didn't leave, he was going to kill me."

"Jesus," Holden breathed.

Both women looked up at him.

"I'm sorry. For everything you've been through."

Edie smiled at him. "I'm sorry for anything I said to you. I know I'm still fuzzy. I'm still a little unsure what's real and what isn't, but I'm sorry."

"You have nothing to apologize for," Holden assured her. "We're just glad you're safe."

"Me, too."

Mackenzie and Edie were sitting on the bed talking when Holden heard a noise downstairs. He told them to stay put and that he'd be right back. There was no lock on the door, but he wasn't going to let anyone get to them.

Holden stepped out into the hallway and looked down. It was still quiet, so he turned his attention to the front door. Daylight was shining through it for the first time in days. Someone was there digging them out.

They were almost free.

11

———

MACKENZIE WATCHED AS THE LAST OF THE SNOW WAS CLEARED from the door. She held her breath, waiting. A piece of her feared the worst and that it was Damon Street there to kill them, but Marcus's face looked through the glass at her, and she let out a sigh of relief that nearly knocked her to her knees.

Holden helped Marcus shove the door open, and the two men introduced themselves, looking to Mackenzie for confirmation that they were who they said they were. When she nodded, Holden let Marcus inside.

"Are you here alone?" Mackenzie asked.

"No. I have an entire crew with me, but I told them I'd check on you guys. I have a small group I trust that will take Edie." He looked past them. "Where is she?"

"Upstairs. She's still pretty weak. I gave her fluids, but we were somewhat limited on supplies. She hasn't eaten much in days, maybe longer." Holden led the way toward the stairs.

"Why is it so damn cold in here?"

Holden pointed to the door that was covered in a blanket. "Hallway collapsed. Door isn't sealed. I did the best I could."

"Very inventive." Marcus nodded his approval.

Holden shrugged. His ears turned pink as he led the way up the stairs. He was definitely not used to being complimented on his quick thinking or intelligence.

Mackenzie followed the men, but Holden stepped back and held Marcus back to allow Mackenzie to go into the bunk room first. Mackenzie opened the door and smiled at her new friend.

"We're finally getting out of here," Mackenzie told her, closing the door on the two men.

"We are? Are you sure?"

Mackenzie nodded. "The police captain I told you about is here to take you to rehab. He has a small team he trusts that's going to keep you safe. No one else will know you're here or ever were here."

"Are you sure?"

Mackenzie nodded. "Positive. I trust him. Completely."

Edie sucked in a breath and nodded. "Okay."

"I'll help you get dressed. It's freezing outside this room."

Edie hadn't been up much in the days she'd been there. Trips to the bathroom were really it for her. She was unsteady on her feet and nearly fell onto the bed once she stood. Her legs were bare, but she wore an oversized sweatshirt Holden had found for her. There was a clean change of clothes on the bed Mackenzie was supposed to sleep on.

The two of them worked together to get Edie dressed. She didn't have shoes besides the heels she was wearing when she arrived, so Mackenzie gave Edie the sneakers she'd been wearing.

"You need something, too."

Mackenzie waved off her concern and said she'd be

okay.

"I can't take your shoes."

"I'm going to take yours," Mackenzie teased her.

Edie shivered. "You can have them. The man who kept me gave them to me. Do me a favor and burn them when you're done with them."

Mackenzie grimaced and nodded. "I will."

Edie was finally ready to go, so Mackenzie opened the door for Holden and Marcus to come in. The two of them helped her down the stairs and outside to the waiting vehicle. It was nondescript but loaded with people who all looked at Marcus with respect.

Before they took off, Marcus got out of the vehicle and walked back over to Mackenzie and Holden. "She'd like you to visit. She asked me to give you all the information about where she is and what's going on. Once she's secure, I'll be in touch. Is that okay?"

Mackenzie nodded, tears choking her throat. "Yes," she whispered.

Marcus squeezed Mackenzie's shoulder and nodded, then turned back to the vehicle. He climbed in beside Edie and the SUV pulled out. Mackenzie watched until it disappeared from view.

"Are you okay?" Holden asked.

Mackenzie nodded, even though she felt far from okay.

"Sir? Ma'am? We've been asked to take you over to the call center. Do you have everything you need?" a young officer asked them. His gaze slid down Mackenzie and flinched at the four-inch heels that definitely did not go with her outfit, but he didn't say anything about them.

Holden looked at Mackenzie and raised a brow. She nodded. "We're ready."

The young officer led them across the shoveled driveway

outside the building. It was icy and slippery, especially in heels Mackenzie wasn't used to wearing. Holden kept his arm around her waist to steady her whenever she lost her balance.

The officer opened the door for them at the entrance to the call center. He followed them inside and moved to the side to join another group.

Mackenzie blinked at the place she'd worked for years and almost didn't recognize it. It felt like a lifetime had passed since they'd been there. It all looked exactly the same, but Mackenzie wasn't. She'd done some real good. She'd helped save a woman.

"Are you—?"

"Holden! Oh, my God! You're back. I was so worried about you! How are you? Oh, you're safe. I'm so happy nothing *happened*."

Isabel.

She rushed over to Holden and threw herself into his arms. He caught her with his hands on her waist, and she smirked at Mackenzie over Holden's shoulder. Isabel pressed herself tighter to Holden and rubbed her breasts against his chest.

And he did nothing. He hugged her and said nothing.

Mackenzie waited a beat for him to push Isabel away or tell her to let go or something, but he just stood there and held her. He embraced the woman he'd insisted for days that he wasn't involved with.

Fucking liar.

Mackenzie knew exactly what Isabel was implying with her comment, and rubbing herself all over Holden like a cat marking her territory was more than Mackenzie was willing to take. Vomit rose up in her throat. She'd spent the last two nights wrapped in his arms, telling herself she could trust him and that he wasn't like the other men she'd know, but the first time they were back with their coworkers, he proved Mackenzie wrong and let Isabel act like they were still a thing.

Mackenzie turned and walked away. She didn't have time or energy for games, and if Isabel wanted to play one, she could play by herself. Mackenzie was done. Done with Isabel, and done with Holden.

HOLDEN TRIED to push Isabel away, but she held on tighter, practically climbing him as he attempted to extricate himself from her grip.

"What are you doing?" he hissed in her ear.

"I was so worried about you. I thought you were going to die over there with that murderer," Isabel proclaimed.

For a second, Holden thought Isabel meant Edie, but then he remembered Mackenzie's past. No one who knew Mackenzie could ever think she would be violent, even after her confession to Holden that she wouldn't hesitate to kill Damon Street. That man had done more harm than most, so Holden understood the desire to see him dead and gone. But that didn't mean Mackenzie would kill for sport.

Out of the corner of his eye, Holden saw Mackenzie walking away, head held high and shoulders stiff. She was hurt. Understandably. Isabel only said what she did to hurt Mackenzie.

Holden didn't like being the bad guy, and Isabel knew that. Shoving her away would make him look cruel, but he wasn't going to appease Isabel's fragile ego and allow Mackenzie to be hurt in the process.

He adjusted his grip on Isabel and shoved her off him.

She stumbled at the sudden jolt and flailed before she lost her balance and fell backward. She landed hard on her ass, a squeak of indignation and pain popping out of her before she looked up at Holden with wide eyes and a sneer.

"What the hell was that for?"

"We're done. We've been done. I told you we were done. I want nothing to do with you. And if you say one more thing about Mackenzie, or imply once more that she could have harmed anyone, I'll call a lawyer and sue you for slander."

"Only if it's not true."

Rage tightened Holden's hands into fists. He'd never considered hitting a woman before, but the bitch at his feet was one who might earn that honor. He couldn't believe he fell for her. That he once thought her beauty was something to be desired. She was gorgeous, but she was hideous on the inside. She made him regret ever sleeping with her or thinking maybe there could have been something there. Those thoughts were long gone.

"Are you going to hit me, Holden?" Isabel asked, her voice rising. She injected fear into it, drawing attention to herself on the ground.

Holden towered over her, his fists clenched and his jaw tense.

Their coworkers turned to watch them without disguising their interest in the argument. Their eyes widened when they saw Holden's position of power over Isabel, the innocent woman cowering on the floor.

"You're not fucking worth it. Stay away from me. And stay away from Mackenzie."

Holden stalked away from Isabel as she burst into fake tears that did nothing but earn her sympathy for the lies she was telling.

He hated himself for not seeing it before. She was a master at hiding who she was, and at getting others to want her. Either as a friend or in bed. He fell for it, hook, line, and sinker.

MACKENZIE WAS ready to get the hell out of there. She wanted her own shower, her own bed, and a few days alone.

She caught the stares and worried looks her coworkers threw her way. Some were new enough that they didn't know about her past. Others had likely forgotten they were working alongside an accused killer.

Hot tears stung her eyes, but she refused to let them fall. She wouldn't give Isabel the victory. That woman was vile, but everyone loved her. Including Holden.

A crowd gathered where Mackenzie left Holden and Isabel. He was probably proposing or something. Ugh. Mackenzie hated herself for thinking for even one minute that she might have had a chance with Holden. She was not the woman the hot guy wanted. She was the sidekick. The one no one remembered after the story was over.

She dug her handbag out of her desk and locked it again. Her phone was almost dead, and her car was likely buried under snow taller than her, but she was ready to get the hell out of there. She'd figure out the rest later.

Mackenzie stopped in Amanda's office and told her she was heading out. Amanda asked how she was and raised an eyebrow at the shoes that were clearly not Mackenzie's. Mackenzie didn't bother to explain and teetered her way toward the door when Amanda said she could go.

She almost made it, too.

"Mackenzie!" Holden's footsteps hurried down the

hallway behind her.

Mackenzie tried to move faster, but the fucking heels were not cooperating. Her ankles twisted and turned, nearly sending her into the wall three times before Holden caught up to her and grabbed her arm.

"Hey. I was calling you."

Mackenzie laughed mirthlessly. "Yeah. When no one's around. You should be worried about being alone with me."

"Why would I be worried?"

"I heard what your girlfriend said. Everyone did. She made sure of it."

"Isabel is a bitch who only cares about what others think of her. She pulled that stunt because she wants to be the center of attention, but we were. We were the ones trapped over there, and she was jealous."

"Jealous?" Mackenzie scoffed. She didn't believe a word of it.

Holden nodded. "That's how she is. She doesn't actually care about anyone but herself. Her only goal is to make sure as many people as possible are paying attention to her. If that means throwing herself at me when we get back, she's game. If that means lying about you, she'll definitely do that. She doesn't care who she hurts as long as she comes out on top."

"You sure know how to pick the good ones," Mackenzie said sarcastically.

Holden stepped forward. He tucked a strand of hair behind her ear and trailed his fingertips across her jaw. "My taste has definitely improved."

"From the psycho to the killer. Some would disagree."

"I don't care what anyone else thinks. I care about you, Mackenzie. I ended things with Isabel because she didn't believe in me. She thought I was too dumb to chase a dream. She is happy to use her looks to get what she wants, but that's not me. I didn't think that was you either."

His words hit a little too close to home. Mackenzie prided herself on not caring what others thought. She was the woman accused of killing her best friend. She had her name dragged through enough mud to fill the Niagara Gorge. She hated people who listened to the gossip and the word of others instead of making their own decisions. She'd been the victim of it too many times.

And instead of learning from her own past and not being that way, she was doing the same damn thing as the people who threw her to the wolves and believed Peter.

"It's not me," Mackenzie admitted. "Not the me I want to be."

Holden tipped her jaw up. "It's not the you I like. You're kind and compassionate. You see what's beneath the outer shell of a person. You didn't judge Edie, you became her friend. That's who I want to be with. Not someone like Isabel."

"You want to be with Edie?" Mackenzie asked. She was confused. If he wanted Edie, why was he looking at her like she was the one he craved?

Holden chuckled. "No, I don't want to be with Edie. You, Mackenzie. What happened between us over there? That's not it for me. I would have walked in here with your hand in mine if Isabel hadn't gotten in between us."

"She did that on purpose."

"Trust me, I know. She hates the idea of us. I don't know why, but—"

"Because you ended things. She can't handle that."

Holden shrugged and nodded. "You're probably right. And for that, I'm sorry you're in the middle. But I won't let her hurt you."

"I'm not worried about Isabel. She's nothing compared to the evil out there."

Mackenzie shivered. Edie's story about being taken from one house and locked in another had been running through Mackenzie's head all day. It meant wherever Edie was being held was close to where Mackenzie worked. Close enough that Damon, or whoever was holding Edie, was right there every day when Mackenzie went to work and left. They could have been watching her. She could have been an easy target for them.

So why did they take Edie, who had a cousin and wasn't unwanted, and not Mackenzie?

"Mackenzie?" Holden asked. His tone suggested it wasn't the first time he'd called her name.

"Hmm? Sorry."

"Are you okay?"

She shook her head. Isabel, Edie, Damon. It was all a lot. She didn't think Isabel was dangerous, just mean. And even that was almost a stretch. She was lonely. She was heartbroken. Maybe she was in love with Holden. And instead of having him return that affection, he ended things.

And to keep up appearances, she pretended it didn't get to her or acted like they were still together.

Mackenzie felt bad for Isabel. Not that it made her think Isabel was any less of a bitch, but Isabel didn't have anyone in her corner. She wouldn't be forgotten. She definitely wasn't unwanted. But would she have someone to lean on if she really needed someone?

Did Mackenzie?

She looked up at Holden and thought she might. Not only that, but she wanted to. For the first time in years, she wanted to not be unwanted. She wanted to have someone to call when she didn't feel like having dinner alone. She wanted someone who would be there for her. No matter what.

"Are you okay?" he asked again.

Mackenzie nodded. She was done worrying about what others thought. She'd spent a long time hiding who she was so she didn't have to deal with the ridicule and pain, but she was done. It was going to come no matter what, so she needed to stop hiding herself.

"I will be," she admitted to Holden.

A grin lifted his lips, one corner at a time, until he grinned widely at her. "Yeah?"

She nodded.

"So, what are you doing tonight? Any chance I can take you out on a date?"

Mackenzie laughed. "A date? We just spent forty-eight hours together with no breaks."

"And I'd do it again in a heartbeat. Are you saying you're sick of me?"

Mackenzie shook her head slowly. "Nope."

"Good. Then... date?"

Mackenzie looked past Holden to their coworkers, shamelessly watching them. She smirked at him and pulled him down for a kiss.

His hands immediately closed around her body, hauling her against him. He tilted his head and licked his way into her mouth. She moaned softly, taking a small step forward.

Slowly, the sounds of the office returned, and Mackenzie eased back. Holden's eyes stayed closed for a long moment after their lips separated. He smiled and drew a deep breath.

"Was that a yes?"

Mackenzie breathed a laugh. "Yeah, I'd say that was definitely a yes."

12

———

THE WORLD OUTSIDE THE STATION WAS SHUT DOWN. IT amazed Mackenzie as she drove home to see how few things were open. Restaurants, stores, even gas stations were closed. It was like the city had turned into a ghost town.

When she arrived at her apartment complex, the parking lots were a mess. Plows had been through, but most of the parking spaces were occupied with cars buried under six or more feet of snow. She found a spot toward the back of her the lot closest to her building and hoped she was close to the lines she needed to be in.

Nothing in her apartment looked out of place. The stale scent told her no one had been there while she was gone. She cracked open a window to let a little fresh air inside and sat on the couch.

She was exhausted.

Mackenzie jolted upright, something waking her from what had been a sound sleep. She shivered, realizing she'd left the window open and fallen asleep.

Her phone. That's what woke her up. She grabbed it from her handbag and checked the text while she closed the window and locked it. She smiled when she saw Holden's name on the screen. He'd insisted they trade numbers before they left work so they could solidify plans for their date that night.

> Not sure what's open for our first date. The city is pretty quiet.

> I noticed that too. We can reschedule for another day.

> If you want to, we can, but I was going to ask if you were up for coming to my place and I can cook. Or I can come to you.

> I don't have anything here to cook.

> Are you up for coming to my place? I can pick you up.

> There's no reason for you to pick me up. I'll come to you. What time?

> Six?

> Gives me time to jump in the shower. I passed out on the couch. See you soon.

> Tease. Now I'm going to be thinking about you in the shower.

Mackenzie gaped at her phone. He was flirting with her. And picturing her naked. She'd never had a guy do that.

> Did I scare you off?

> No. Just surprised me. I'm not used to that.

> Used to what?

Someone wanting me.

You're wanted, Mackenzie. Trust me.

Feeling's mutual.

Good. See you soon.

Yep.

Mackenzie smiled as she changed out of the borrowed clothes she was wearing and got in the shower. She cleaned herself quickly, shaved, and got out. She felt better after a hot shower. Awake and ready for her date with Holden.

It was still freezing cold outside, so she went with comfortable for her outfit. Jeans she loved paired with a plum sweater that was so soft it felt like she wasn't wearing anything. She added a pair of boots that were warm and cozy.

Before Mackenzie left, she saw Edie's heels. She'd kicked them off when she walked into her apartment, and there they were at the door. Mocking her. She stared at them, knowing she couldn't actually burn them.

Mackenzie picked up the heels and carried them to her trashcan. She stuffed them inside, glaring at the heels that marked Edie. They were a symbol of ownership. The whole thing made Mackenzie sick.

She pushed it all out of her mind. There was nothing Mackenzie could do at the moment. She didn't know where Damon was. She would figure it out, but until she did, she was going to live her life. It was what Jaclyn would have wanted. Mackenzie knew that, even though she'd always resisted it.

For the first time in years, Mackenzie wanted to enjoy life.

Holden lived in a nice apartment complex in downtown. It wasn't close enough to overlook the Falls, but it was close enough to walk there if he wanted. It was miles nicer than her place. She had to tamp down her unease at going there. Feeling like she didn't belong.

As soon as she knocked, Holden opened the door, like he'd been waiting for her. She smiled and stepped inside, her nose leading the way as much as the rest of her.

"It smells amazing," she admitted. Her stomach rumbled loudly.

Holden chuckled. "Thanks. My mom didn't like to cook and my dad was always gone, so I became the family cook when I was young. It relaxes me. No one ever told me what to do in the kitchen."

"Wow. I just..."

"What?"

Mackenzie smiled up at him. "I never would have pictured you with a tough life. I see you with a silver spoon."

"I can't say it was tough. I know I had a lot of privilege other people didn't have. Money was abundant, but love was nonexistent. I've always felt like I don't know how to actually care about people because I never learned."

"I think you're pretty good at caring. You might not have learned from your parents, but you show people every day that you care."

"Thank you," he whispered. His Adam's apple bobbed as he swallowed. He pressed his lips into a smile and drew a breath.

Mackenzie smiled up at him and resisted the urge to lean in and kiss him. She needed to take things slowly. Not that she wanted to, but she didn't want to jump into sex and find out later Holden wasn't who she thought he was.

"Do you want a glass of wine?" Holden blurted. He

turned away to go toward the kitchen, already predicting an answer.

Mackenzie breathed a little easier knowing he was nervous, too. It didn't matter that he'd seen her half-naked and made her moan his name as she came. "I don't drink," she confessed.

He stopped and faced her. "I didn't realize. Sorry I asked."

She shook her head. "I'm not an alcoholic. I... Drinking makes me feel vulnerable."

So many things in her life went back to the night Jaclyn was killed. They'd all been drinking the night before. The police tested Mackenzie, and her blood alcohol level was above the legal limit. They used it as one more piece of false evidence against her.

"I understand that. I'm not a big drinker either. But I'm..." Holden's voice trailed off.

Mackenzie moved into his path and waited for him to meet her gaze. "I'm nervous, too."

He smiled and wrapped his arms around her. It was the first time he'd touched her since she'd arrived. She'd started to second guess being there after he'd kept his distance, but she finally felt like it was going to be okay. "It's been a long time since I've been on a date."

"Oh." He tensed against her, a move so small she would have missed it if she wasn't in his arms. He pulled back, releasing her as she spoke again.

"And even before that, I didn't like the men I dated as much as I like you."

His grin lit up his entire face.

"Stop looking at me like that," she said, her face warming as she tried to hide from him.

Holden reached for her hand. "Thank you for coming here tonight."

"Thank you for inviting me."

Holden pulled her closer and lifted his other hand to her cheek. He hesitated just long enough to catch her gaze. Mackenzie leaned in, closing the distance between them and pressing her lips to his.

Holden's fingers curled against her cheek, drawing her closer. His breath filled his lungs, putting his chest in contact with hers. Everything about the kiss felt new, different, special. Like it was a first kiss, even though it wasn't. This kiss wasn't about sex or desire or lust they couldn't stop from pulling them together. This kiss was about something more. Something deeper. Something that made Mackenzie's eyes prick with unshed tears and her heart fill with something she'd never known before.

She inhaled a sharp breath. Holden gentled the kiss, pulling back from her in a way that felt reluctant. He pressed his forehead to hers, his eyes closed, and breathed.

"I'm really happy you're here," he whispered.

"I am, too."

He squeezed her hand once more, then backed away. "I'm going to burn dinner if I keep kissing you."

Mackenzie chuckled and followed him into the kitchen. A pan simmered on the stove, the scent of garlic and spices drawing her closer. Her stomach rumbled again.

"Do you like shrimp? I should have asked. I'm not very good at this, apparently."

"You're perfect," Mackenzie admitted, her cheeks warming when she realized what she said.

Holden chuckled. "Hopefully perfect for you."

Mackenzie grinned. "Yes, I like shrimp. For future reference, no allergies. I'm not a big fan of tomatoes, but I don't mind them in things. I tend to pick around them."

"No tomatoes in this, so I think we're good. It's almost ready." He tapped the spoon on the side of the pan and moved to one of the cabinets. He grabbed two bowls and set them on the counter, then opened another cabinet and retrieved two glasses. "Water okay?"

"Yeah, water is good."

He moved around the kitchen like he was a part of it. Mackenzie had never been a fan of cooking and tolerated it as a means to an end, but Holden almost made cooking look like it was fun.

He turned off the stove and served dinner. He set both plates on the opposite side of the island that separated his kitchen from his living area.

"Sorry. I don't actually have a dining room."

"I usually eat on my couch."

Holden laughed. "Living alone can be tough. You get into routines that most people would frown on."

"I think I'm done living my life worrying about how others think of me."

Holden's brows shot up. He glanced at Mackenzie. "You don't seem like you ever did that."

She nodded. "All the time. Usually it led me to hide because I didn't want to be faced with public opinion. I'm done hiding."

A slow smile lifted his lips. "Does that mean for our next date I can take you out to a restaurant and show you off?"

"If you can find one that's open."

"I'll find one. If it means I get to go out with you again."

"Shouldn't you see how this date goes before you start planning a second date?"

He shook his head. "I already know this date is going to

be amazing because I'm here with you. That's all I want right now."

Mackenzie smiled and nodded. "Sounds good to me."

They ate their dinner and talked about work. Holden asked more about Damon, but they quickly changed the subject. Neither of them wanted to talk about him. Not after spending days thinking about him.

Mackenzie insisted on helping Holden clean the kitchen, then he led her to the couch and asked, "Can I talk you into staying to watch a movie?"

"It depends what kind of movie you want to watch."

"I think I could go for a comedy tonight. If you're up for that."

Mackenzie nodded. "Sounds perfect."

Holden found a movie neither of them had seen and started it. Mackenzie laughed and let herself get lost in the story that kept her entertained and distracted. It was a good feeling after being hyper alert for days.

When the movie ended, they were closer than when the movie started. The credits rolled up the screen, and Holden reached for her hand.

"Thank you for coming over tonight."

"I had a lot of fun."

"I'm not trying to kick you out."

She smiled. "I know, but I feel like I should go."

"I understand."

She studied him carefully for a minute. There was no hint of disappointment, which made her wonder. "Do you want me to go?"

"No, but we've had a long few days. I felt a little selfish asking you to come here. All I wanted to do after I left work today was be home. I wanted to see you, but I was looking forward to being home. You might not feel the same, but I don't blame you at all if you are ready to get home and just be in your own space."

She looked at him and wondered how he saw the pieces of her she'd kept hidden for so long. "Thank you for understanding."

"Any chance I can kiss you before you go?"

She smiled. "I have a feeling that could be arranged."

He moved closer to her on the couch and cupped her cheek. He slowly drew them together until the anticipation almost made her crazy. But she waited, knowing it would be worth it.

He tasted her, a tiny little kiss that felt like a sample. His lips pressed to hers over and over, taking little pieces of her and leaving pieces of him. With each breath, she wanted him more and more.

When he finally parted his lips and licked against hers, she nearly wept with relief. His tongue rolled against hers, once more sampling her instead of devouring her. There was no rush, no demand, no urgency. It was like they had forever to kiss.

Forever.

The word rolled around in Mackenzie's mind as she kissed Holden. Could she really imagine forever with him? With anyone? She hadn't given herself that luxury, and a man like Holden would never have been on her radar. He was too perfect for her. Someone others would look at and wonder why he was with her.

But he never made her feel that way. He made her feel like she was special. She was the one he wanted. Not Isabel, not anyone else. Just her.

Holden eventually softened the kiss. He pulled Mackenzie against him and held her. His heart hammered in his chest, under her ear. He was just as gone as she was. And that was a strange but wonderful feeling.

DAMON STOOD on the street smoking a cigarette. It was an old vice he'd given up long ago, but one he picked up again when he was a wanted man, unable to stand on his own two feet.

He was going to kill Trevor.

More than wanting to kill Raina for what she did to him, Trevor was working his way to first place in Damon's book. He still hadn't figured out how the twat-waffle found where he was hiding Edie and got her out of that room, but Trevor would pay for rescuing his whore.

And so would she.

There was a part of Damon that knew he was lucky. Trevor could have slit his throat when he took Edie out from under Damon's fucking nose, but he didn't. He just stole the bitch and ran. Like the fucking coward he was.

Damon wasn't a coward. He wasn't going to back down. Not when he had a plan. A mission. A reason to keep fighting.

Lights went out in the house, and Damon stubbed out his cigarette. He knew it was risky to go in there, but he had to prove his value. Once he did that, the boss would have no choice but to bring him back and kick Trevor out of his assumed place of power.

Damon kept to the shadows and moved silently across the yard. Where headquarters was a fortress, this house was nondescript and barely something anyone would think could be holding the boss of a crime family.

The easy option was to torch the place, flush the boss

out, and kill everyone else, but Damon wasn't looking to kill everyone. He was looking to send a message. A message that would prove he was worthy.

Every door was wired with a camera and an alarm. The ground-floor windows were all the same. Getting inside would take effort. But Damon hadn't been watching the boss for months to give up now.

The trellis on the side of the house was centered between two windows, windows that looked out from the kitchen. It wasn't the most sturdy thing ever, but Damon knew it would hold his weight. And he knew the window above him and to the right would be his best option for an access point.

He climbed soundlessly, the rustle of leaves blending in with the light breeze blowing. It was colder than fucking hell, and the trellis was covered in snow from the feet that had dumped on the city, but Damon's gut burned with fury and a need for revenge.

At the top of the trellis, Damon ran out of spots to reach. The window was almost out of his reach, but he hadn't come so far to give up. He was going to make it work.

He balanced carefully on the top, knowing his time was running out. If he slipped, they'd find him. If he made noise, they'd find him. If he fucked up in the slightest bit, they'd find him. None of those were options.

He reached for the window, his fingertips landing on the sill. It was wet and covered in a few inches of snow. Everything was covered in snow. But this was his chance.

Damon brushed the snow from the windowsill and grabbed on. He'd broken into more than his fair share of second-story windows and had the biceps to support himself and the core strength to keep his body from slamming into the side of the house. It took no more than a few seconds to lift himself up and shove at the window.

Unlocked. Just like he left it months ago.

Damon smiled to himself and pushed the window up. He knew no one would notice the window being unlocked. And he knew it might come in handy as the Company started to crumble beneath his feet.

He stepped into the house without a sound and paused, listening for anyone coming. Guards, the boss, a visitor.

It was deadly silent.

Damon knew the house well after having been a guest in it many times. The last boss trusted Damon and allowed him to stay there more than once. The current boss didn't share the same feelings and kept Damon out most of the time.

He tiptoed to the door, his steps careful to avoid making any noise in the old house. The snow outside would show everyone exactly how he'd gained access to the house, so this was his only shot.

He pulled the knife from his belt. He flipped it in his hand, the blade along his wrist, ready to strike. It would be so easy to eliminate the boss, to take control of the company by force, but Damon didn't want it that way. He wanted the boss to hand it over. To beg for mercy and surrender it all to Damon.

Damon knew Trevor's money would be a benefit to the company, but he'd find his own way to shore things up. Taking money from Trevor wasn't an option. Especially not when Trevor would be dead.

Damon retrieved the note and the rose from his inside pocket. He pierced through the stem and into the note, then pressed his knife silently into the drywall next to the boss's bedroom door. There was no way to miss it, or the message he was sending.

He was close enough to kill the boss if he wanted. But he chose not to. He would be rewarded for that.

And then he could move on to the next phase of his plan. Eliminate the competition and retrieve what had been taken from him.

13

———

A full week had passed since the storm and Mackenzie was starting to get back into her normal routine. Normal now included Saturday trips to visit Edie at rehab and dates with Holden, but her new normal was better than her old normal.

Edie was doing really well and feeling good. Her cravings had mostly passed and her counselors were confident she'd be able to live a normal life again. It helped that Edie hadn't chosen the drugs on her own and that she had no interest in going back to that world.

Things with Holden were going well, too. He'd cooked for her again, and they talked almost every day. Mackenzie couldn't help but smile whenever she thought about him. Their schedules didn't always match up, but when they did, they would try to talk before or after their shifts. The hallway hadn't been repaired yet, which meant they couldn't meet in the break room, and for the first time, Mackenzie found she missed those not-so-coincidental moments.

Mackenzie sat at her desk and smiled. Holden was

finishing his shift in a few hours and wanted to take Mackenzie out. Their first official date, he said.

Mackenzie's first official date in years. She was nervous and excited and really looking forward to it.

She signed into the system and resumed her search for Damon. When she wasn't answering calls, she was digging into the man, and finding more and more about him. And some of his associates. Edie mentioned Trevor, so Mackenzie added him to her list and found more calls. The network and the history on them was terrifying.

The phone rang and Mackenzie closed the program she was using for research to focus on the call.

"Nine-one-one. What is your emergency?"

"I was in a car accident. I need help. Please."

"Can you tell me where you are, sir?"

The man on the phone huffed like his breathing was labored. "One-ninety. Heading toward the Falls. My family is with me."

Mackenzie put in the information to send a rescue unit toward them. "How many people are in the car?"

"My wife and my son. He's three. And he's not crying. He's always crying."

"Someone will be there soon and they will do everything they can. How is your wife? Is she awake?"

"Honey? Can you hear me?" He groaned. "She's not answering me. She's bleeding. Her head."

"Can you tell me what happened? How did you get into an accident?"

"Someone... cut me off. Icy roads. I hit my brakes when they cut in front of me and just... lost control."

"I'm so sorry. The police will look into it. Hey, what's your name?"

"Steven. My wife is Erica."

"Hi, Steven. What's your son's name?"

"Jerry. After my dad."

"You said he's three? Is he your first?"

"Yeah. He's a great kid. He hates the car because he can't see what's going on. Pediatrician said keep him rear-facing. We tried mirrors but he just cries. Says he wants to see us."

"That can't be easy." Mackenzie saw the progress of the ambulance and knew they were almost to Steven and his family. "Do you see the ambulance yet, Steven? They should be there very soon."

Steven grunted again as a knock came through the line. "Yeah. They're here. My son! Check on my son and my wife."

Voices came through the phone that Mackenzie couldn't understand, but she knew it meant help had arrived. "Steven, do you want me to hang up so you can speak to the paramedics and police?"

"Yeah. Okay. Thank you. Thank you so much."

"You're welcome, Steven."

Mackenzie hung up the phone and breathed a steadying breath. Help had arrived. Hopefully, they would all be okay. Unfortunately, Mackenzie knew the driver that caused the accident would never be held accountable for it. The system sucked.

Two more calls came in and Mackenzie helped a woman with a possible gas leak in her house and a man who was reporting a fire on the east side of the city. Mackenzie sent crews to both calls and was feeling good about the end of her day. Only one more hour until she was done.

The clock ticked by as Mackenzie did more digging into Damon and Trevor. She checked the time and saw she was down to her last fifteen minutes when her phone rang again.

"Nine-one-one. What is your emergency?"

"I need help. Please. My boyfriend... I think he broke my arm, probably a rib, too."

Mackenzie started the report for a crew to be sent. "Can you tell me your address?"

"Six-one-nine Springwood Avenue."

Mackenzie added the information and sent it to a crew with a warning about the boyfriend. "Are you somewhere safe right now?"

"Yes. He left. He was going out with friends. He got mad at me for wanting to go with him. I made the mistake of saying one of his friends was nice."

Mackenzie tried to hold back her anger. "That shouldn't be something that upsets him so much. And he should never hurt you."

"Yeah, I agree." She sighed heavily. "I'm not from here. I moved here to be with him and now I just feel trapped." Her voice wobbled as she spoke.

"I'm Mackenzie. What's your name?"

"Jill."

"Hi, Jill. I know someone who can help you. She runs a local shelter and will get you from the hospital and protect you until you can get somewhere else."

Jill sucked in a breath. "Really?"

"Yes. If you want me to reach out to her, I will ask her to meet you at the hospital."

Jill sniffed, then choked on a sob. "Thank you. Yes, I'd really like that. Rick wasn't always like this, but it's not the first time. I feel stuck. I almost didn't call you, but it hurts just to breathe. To move. And I knew I needed help."

"You'll get it, Jill. I promise you. The woman I'm going to call is Francesca. I'll give her your information. She will meet you there."

"Thank you, Mackenzie. I really appreciate it."

"You're welcome. Are you able to unlock your door, Jill? The paramedics are almost to you."

Muffled sounds came through the line. She cried out once. "Sorry. I was sitting on the bathroom floor. I'm up now."

"Is Rick still gone?"

She was silent, as if she was listening. "Yeah, I don't hear him. I'm going to the door."

Jill was quiet for a minute. The click of the door unlocking came through the phone. Then Mackenzie heard a man's voice.

"What the fuck are you doing? Who are you talking to?"

"Rick. I thought you left."

The fear in Jill's voice sent shivers down Mackenzie's spine. "Jill. Stay calm. The paramedics are almost there."

"Okay," Jill said.

"Who are you talking to? Is that Harry? You think he's so fucking nice."

A sound echoed through the line, then the phone clattered to the floor. Mackenzie listened as Rick shouted at Jill. Paramedics were pulling up in front of the address now.

"Assailant inside the residence with the victim now. Door is unlocked. Proceed with caution and get her the hell out of there," Mackenzie told whoever was responding to the call.

"Copy," was all she got back.

Mackenzie listened through the phone and heard the knock of the paramedics. They didn't wait long before entering the home since they knew she was inside and in danger.

"You can't walk into my home," Rick barked at them.

"Your girlfriend called for help," another voice said. "We're here to take her to the hospital."

"No, you're not. She doesn't need help. You're fine. Aren't you, Jill?"

Mackenzie waited with her breath held. She knew how this could go. She whispered for Jill to be rescued. For her to break free.

"He hit me. He broke my arm and a rib, I think. And when he heard me calling for help, he hit me again. I'd like to press charges against him. Now."

"I'll fucking kill you, you bitch!" Rick roared.

Rick's grunt was the next thing Mackenzie heard, then someone reading him his rights. Mackenzie breathed a sigh of relief. Jill was safe, and Rick was going away.

The paramedics took Jill out of the house, and Mackenzie hung up. She immediately called Captain Patrick.

"Patrick."

"Hi, this is Mackenzie."

"Do you have something new for me?"

"Not right now, but I need your help. Actually, your wife's help. If that's okay."

"Are you okay?"

"Yes, but I just took a call from a woman who wasn't. She's safe now, but she's on her way to the hospital and her boyfriend was read his rights. Her name is Jill, his is Rick. And she needs a place to stay for a while. She thinks she has a broken arm and rib."

"We'll take care of it," Captain Patrick said. His voice was firm, angry. "She doesn't deserve that."

"No, she doesn't. I told her to expect Francesca."

"Thank you, Mackenzie. We know not everyone is willing to get help, and the ones that are don't always know where to go. Thank you for reaching out."

"Thank you, Captain. I'll be in touch again, I'm sure."

He sighed. "I wish that wasn't true, but we both know it is. Have a good night."

"You, too."

Mackenzie hung up and let out the breath she'd been holding. She was thankful she didn't get more calls like that, and thankful she now had someone to reach out to when the caller was receptive to help. She would save more women with Francesca's help.

Mackenzie checked the time and saw she was a few minutes over. She logged out of the system and locked up her station. She smiled when she thought about her night and her upcoming date with Holden.

Things between them had been very tame since the storm. Mackenzie wanted him, but she was ready for more. It was right. He was right.

At home, she changed into skinny jeans that molded to her curves and a long top that exposed a hint of her cleavage. She added light makeup and shook her hair free of the ponytail she'd had it in all day. Her gentle waves fell around her shoulders and looked good for once. She grabbed a simple pair of gold hoops and the diamond necklace Jaclyn gave her for her twenty-first birthday, and she was ready.

She drew a breath and realized she was excited for her date. Even after the call with Jill, Mackenzie was happy about seeing Holden.

Maybe she trusted him more than she thought.

HOLDEN KNOCKED on Mackenzie's door at exactly seven o'clock. He'd been there for fifteen minutes, but he didn't want to be too early, so he forced himself to wait.

And damn, was it worth the wait.

Mackenzie opened the door and smiled at him. She was stunning. Her hair was loose and flowing, like it was when they were trapped together. Her eyes looked even bigger than usual. The black top she wore scooped low on her breasts and made his mouth water.

He wasn't sure he was going to survive the night without begging her to let him have a taste of her.

"Hey," she said after a minute.

"You're gorgeous," he answered. Holden ran a hand through his hair. "Sorry. I... Hi."

Mackenzie chuckled softly and reached behind the door. "Should we head out?"

Holden nodded, not trusting his mouth to agree. His dick strained against his zipper, begging to push her back into the apartment and forget all about dinner and have her instead.

But he couldn't. He promised himself he would wait until she was ready for whatever came next. And he wasn't going back on that promise.

Holden opened Mackenzie's door for her and waited until she was seated before he closed it and jogged around the front of his Jeep, not wanting to be apart from her for longer than absolutely necessary. He cranked up the vehicle and glanced at her once more.

She was looking at him, too. They smiled at each other, and Holden backed out of the parking space.

"How is it being back at work after the storm?" Holden asked. He hated that he hadn't been able to see her during the day like he used to. The door had been barricaded and sealed so the heat would keep each side warm, but it cut off the two groups.

Mackenzie shrugged and nudged her glasses up. "It's been okay. A lot of people asked what we did for forty-eight hours."

Holden smirked when he thought of their nights together and the way he held her. Mackenzie's cheeks turned pink when he met her gaze.

"I didn't tell them about any of that."

"Or about Edie."

"No," she blurted. "Definitely not."

"What did you tell them?"

"That we talked and cooked and sat around. I said it was boring."

"If they only knew," Holden said. The time they spent together wasn't easy, but they were great days in his book. Days when he didn't have to be the pretty face or anything other than himself. He liked that he could just be Holden with Mackenzie around.

"Yes, well, they never will."

He grinned. "Their loss is my gain. Have you spoken to our roommate?" They'd taken to calling Edie their roommate to make sure no one overheard them and questioned who she was. The name could be enough to alert the wrong person, but no one paid attention when they said something about a roommate.

Mackenzie smiled like a proud mama. "She's doing really well. I saw her on Saturday. It hasn't been long, but she feels good."

"Are you going to see her again?"

She nodded. "They have visiting hours every Saturday. I'm going to go as much as I can."

"Tell her I said hello. I'm really happy to hear she'd doing well."

"I will. She's asked how you're doing. She seems to remember more than we thought she would."

"Like what?"

"That first morning. She knows something was going on."

"I'm not ashamed of that," Holden said, reaching for Mackenzie's hand. "Are you?"

"Of course not. Why would I be?"

Holden shrugged, his old insecurities getting the better of him for a moment. She never made him feel like he couldn't do anything he wanted, and he had no reason to think that would change now.

"Have you looked into flight paramedic training again?" Mackenzie asked.

Holden shook his head. "No. Not since we talked. I'm still undecided about it."

"You won't know until you try it. Do they do ride-alongs, or fly-alongs I guess, like you can do for EMTs?"

"I don't know. They might."

"You should call and find out. See what it's like. Get an idea if it's for you."

"That's not a bad idea."

"If you hate it, you still have a job you love. But if you like it, then you know it'll be worth your time to go through the training."

He nodded. "You're right. Thank you."

They arrived at the restaurant, and Holden held Mackenzie's hand as they walked in. They were seated at a quiet table off to the side. The restaurant wasn't overly crowded, which made it possible to speak and not have to strain to hear each other.

A server took their drink orders and left them to look over the menu. Holden couldn't help looking at Mackenzie and smiling when she mouthed the words to herself.

"Everything looks so good," Mackenzie said.

Holden hadn't stopped watching her and agreed

completely. "Yes, you do. I mean, it does." Heat rose to his cheeks. He didn't want to pressure her.

Mackenzie set her menu down and reached across the table for his hand.

He wound their fingers together and smiled. They both reviewed the menu while holding hands.

When the server came back with their waters, they ordered dinner, then he left them again. Holden and Mackenzie chatted about their pasts a little, him telling her about growing up as a child actor and model with a mother who wanted to push him into the same world she was a part of, and her talking about her family and not feeling connected to anyone until she met Jaclyn. Different paths, but the same result. Loneliness.

Their food arrived just after Holden asked how Mackenzie's day was, and he could tell by the look on her face it wasn't good. When the server confirmed they didn't need anything else, he walked away, and Holden asked his question again.

"Something happened, didn't it?"

Mackenzie looked up at him and nodded. "I had a rough call to end my shift. Another abusive boyfriend. She thought he was gone, but I guess he came back and got violent with her while I was on the phone. Thankfully, help arrived and they took him into custody and got her to the hospital, but it was hard to hear."

"I've reported to some of those calls. I'll never understand how someone can go from caring about someone enough to pursue them or want to be with them to hurting them."

"That's because you're a good man, Holden Cross."

He smiled at her. "Thank you."

Mackenzie stood and leaned toward him. Holden met

her in the middle, cupping her jaw before she sealed her lips over his in a kiss. He ached to pull her in tighter and devour her, but they were in public and he wasn't that big of an ass.

They talked about work and what they did when they weren't working as they ate. When the server asked if they wanted dessert, Mackenzie shook her head. Holden followed suit and asked for the check.

"I can pay for my dinner."

"I invited you out, so I feel it's my place to pay," Holden said.

"I didn't think men like you still existed, Holden."

He grinned. "There aren't many of us. Hopefully, you don't decide to check out another model."

Mackenzie nibbled on her lip and shook her head. "You're the only one I'm checking out these days. I promise you that."

"Same, Mackenzie. Same."

14

———

HOLDEN REACHED FOR HER HAND AS THEY WALKED OUT OF THE restaurant. Mackenzie smiled to herself. She couldn't think of the last time she was on a date with a man. A real man. Her ex-boyfriend was barely old enough to drink when they dated, just like Mackenzie. It was more of a friend she had sex with sometimes. They were college students, and a date night was dinner at the student union with their meal plans and a free movie on campus, or drinking with the rest of their friends. It wasn't a nice dinner out where he held her hand or held the door.

But Holden did both. He checked in with Mackenzie throughout the night and barely stopped touching her. So much that by the time they made it to his Jeep, Mackenzie was wound up tight and in need of a release.

Holden opened the door for her and waited for her to climb in. He closed it and walked around the vehicle, then turned it on and blasted the heat. They sat for a minute while the defrost cleared the windshield.

Mackenzie fiddled with the strap on her handbag and nibbled her lower lip. She thought about inviting him back to her place, but she didn't want to force him to turn her down. He had already when they were trapped, and even though she understood, she wasn't sure if there was more to it. This time, there weren't excuses. Not unless he really just didn't want to have sex with her.

"Are you ready for me to take you home?" Holden asked, startling Mackenzie out of her internal debate.

"No," she blurted.

"Where do you want to go?"

"Your place?"

"Is that a question or an answer, Mackenzie?"

"It's an answer. I... I want you, Holden. I know you're—"

He leaned across the console and stopped her words with a kiss. His tongue plunged between her lips. He sucked on her tongue, and his fingers tightened on her neck, drawing them together.

Mackenzie whimpered, and Holden eased the kiss, keeping his lips to hers.

"You need to be sure, Mack. I want you, but only if you're sure about this. We can go to my place and watch a movie or have a drink or find dessert. I'm not ready for the night to end, but if we end up in my bed, I need to know it's what you want."

"It is, Holden. I want you. Please."

He kissed her hard once more, then pulled back so quickly her head spun. Before she knew what was going on, he'd pulled out of the parking lot and was on the way to his place.

Holden was a man on a mission. His jaw was set and his fingers gripped the steering wheel so tight they turned white. He glanced over at Mackenzie a few times on the drive, and she couldn't help but feel desired.

She was wanted.

It had been a long time since she felt that way. Since she was willing to feel that way. She knew she could have had sex over the years. She tried to date a few times. But she always found the creeps and weirdos. The ones who wanted to know about Jaclyn's death. Who either thought she was guilty and wanted her to share details about how it felt to kill someone or the ones who didn't care who was guilty but wanted to know what it was like to see someone die.

After a few dates like that, Mackenzie stopped trying. She stopped even thinking about dating. She'd only done it because her therapist encouraged it, but once she learned what kind of psychos were out there, Mackenzie stopped.

But Holden was different. He never once asked about Jaclyn. He never gave Mackenzie the feeling he was a sicko. He was just Holden. A nice guy who was odd enough to want Mackenzie.

She looked at him as he drove and smiled. Jaclyn would have adored Holden. He was exactly the kind of guy she always said she'd settle down with one day. Peter wasn't. He was fun and wild, like Jaclyn thought men should be in college. But once they graduated, Jaclyn said she was going to change. She wouldn't party. She would get serious and find a guy who was the same.

Holden was serious. He wasn't someone Mackenzie saw coming, but he was amazing. He made her feel like the person she used to be. The person she wanted to be again.

"We're here," he said, and Mackenzie got the feeling they had been for a minute. The Jeep was already getting colder, and the engine was ticking as it cooled.

"Oh. Sorry."

"Are you sure about this?"

Mackenzie turned to face him and nodded. "I'm very

sure. My hesitation had nothing to do with you and everything to do with getting lost in a memory."

Holden nodded once, then opened his door. Mackenzie followed him, meeting on the sidewalk in front of the vehicle. He reached for her hand again and led her inside to his apartment.

Once inside, Holden locked the door and turned on lights. He set his shoes in the entryway closet and hung his coat inside, then reached for her coat and hung it up, too. Mackenzie unzipped her boots and put them in with Holden's shoes.

It was all very domestic. Like they'd been coming home from dates together for years instead of this being the first time.

"There's no pressure here, Mackenzie. Not now, not ever."

"I know," she whispered. "I'm nervous, but that doesn't mean I don't want this."

"Why don't we sit on the couch for a little while?" He turned toward the couch and reached his hand back for her to go with him.

Mackenzie nodded and gave him her hand. He led them to the living room and turned music on the TV. Mackenzie relaxed almost instantly without the silence surrounding them.

"Can I ask you a question?" he said after a minute.

Mackenzie nodded.

"Why did you agree to go out with me?"

"What?"

Holden smiled at her surprise. "I'm just curious. We don't know each other well, and it was pretty obvious to me when we were trapped together that you hadn't been pining away for me like I was for you. So, why did you agree?"

Mackenzie shrugged and shifted. She pulled her legs up under her and toyed with the seam on the back of the couch cushion. "It's hard for me to know if I can trust someone. Even when I think maybe I can, I always find a reason not to. Sometimes it's legitimate and others it's all in my head, but it's made me not trust my instincts."

"You've been through hell, Mack. I get it."

"You've never made me doubt my instincts. You were always exactly who I thought you were. You were kind and thoughtful. You didn't refuse to help Edie just because she looked like she did, the clothes she was wearing. You kept her secret, and you did everything to help her be okay. And you even tried to leave when I admitted I was worried about spending the night together."

"I would have if I could have."

She nodded. "I know. And all those little things showed me who you are. I still questioned though, and when Isabel... When we got back to the call center, and you walked away from her, I knew I wasn't wrong about you."

"You thought you were, though."

She sucked in a breath. "I did. I thought you chose her. I wanted you to let me walk away."

"What? Why?" Holden's eyes narrowed.

"Because it's easier that way. Because I could convince myself I was right about you all along and I could go about my business and not risk getting hurt."

"I'm not going to hurt you," he said, backing up.

Mackenzie smiled sadly at him. "Maybe not on purpose, but eventually, this will end. You'll find someone else, someone who suits you better. Someone who's outgoing and friendly, who makes you laugh. Someone who is your match."

"Why are you so convinced that can't be you?"

She shrugged. "I don't know if I'll ever be whole again. If I'll ever feel like I can open myself up to someone again."

"Were you in love with Jaclyn?" Holden asked.

Mackenzie shook her head. "Not like that. She was like a sister to me. Closer than anyone I've ever known in my life. If I'd ever had any inclination that I was bisexual or gay, I would have fallen for her in a heartbeat. That's the kind of person she was. You couldn't know Jaclyn and not love her. She was fun and infectious. She would make you laugh even if you were just crying. She was smart, too. She could have done anything she wanted to. And she was taken from the world by a man who was selfish and couldn't handle that she was the center of attention and he wasn't."

"She sounds like an amazing person."

"She really was. She brought out the best in me. She made me the person I was too scared to be before I met her. The person I haven't been since she died."

"Who was that person? Tell me about her." Holden's fingertips teased a strand of Mackenzie's hair.

She leaned into him and let him play with her hair while she spoke. "She was fearless. Growing up, I was quiet because my mom was sick. When she died, I was only eleven, but I understood enough to know she could have lived if she made different choices. My dad was angry for a long time. He tried to convince her to stop smoking, but she would laugh at him. I remember her blowing smoke in his face once. He walked out and didn't come back for two days."

"Was he violent?"

"No. Never. My dad was a good man, still is. But he fell in love with a woman who was destructive and selfish. She loved us, in her way, but her way wasn't good. It was limited and doled out in pieces. When she finally died, I think my dad was relieved she was gone. I think that part of him made him angry, though. He felt guilty for being happy she died, so he shut down. I had no one left, so I shut down. I went to school and got good grades, and when I went to college, I went a little wild with the new freedoms I had. I never got in trouble in high school because I knew my dad would be upset, so I didn't step out of line. In college, it was different. And then I met Jaclyn."

Holden kissed the top of her head and tugged her closer. Mackenzie laid on his chest, listening to his heart beat as he stroked her hair.

"Jaclyn lived in the same dorm as me. She was friends with everyone. We saw each other at a few parties, but then we had a class together our second semester. That was when I realized how smart she was. We worked on a project together and studied together, and she made me want to be better. I went from invisible at home to wild at college, but neither of those people were me. I wanted to be stable. To feel confident in who I was and not feel the need to keep up with everyone else."

"That's not easy to do in college."

"No, it isn't. Jaclyn and I decided to live together our sophomore year. I started to get more serious about college and studied a lot more. We still had fun, but we chose who we had fun with instead of partying with anyone and every-one. We started talking about our futures, careers and life and dreams. She wasn't close to her family, and around that time my dad got remarried, so Jaclyn and I got summer jobs working for a local country club and lived together. Our junior year, we got an apartment off campus so we didn't have to share bathrooms with dozens of other girls and we could have a little more freedom. And then she met Peter."

"He was her boyfriend, right?"

Mackenzie nodded. "Pete lived in our building. Jaclyn invited him to a party we were having, and they started talking more after that. I'd started dating a guy from one of my classes, so Jaclyn and I weren't spending as much time together. We would block out a few days every week to see each other, but after a while, Pete got frustrated. He had something planned one of those nights and was mad at her. I told her it was no big deal to change our plans, but she refused. Said she wasn't going to let him or any man control her. I laughed and boosted her up and we drank that night and chastised men in general."

"I can't say I'd have disagreed with you. He could have asked if she had plans, but to expect it and get angry screams of unstable."

"If only we'd had that foresight."

Holden nodded and squeezed her tight.

"The night he killed her, the three of us were hanging out at the apartment. We cooked dinner and watched a movie. We had a few drinks. That's not true. We had a lot of drinks. We'd just finished midterms, and we were relaxing. I fell asleep on the couch, and they left me there. Something woke me up a while later, and I got up to use the bathroom. Her bedroom door was open a little bit, and I saw him in there. He was pacing. She was on the bed, and it looked like he was talking to her. She laughed at something, and he grabbed this candle she had on her desk. It was one of those three-wick candles in a glass jar. He smashed it against her head. Over and over. She fought back, but not for long."

"Jesus."

"I hurried into my room and grabbed my phone. I pretended to be asleep, then I heard the door to our apartment close. My heart was still pounding, but I had to take the chance and call. I didn't know if she was alive or dead, but I knew I had to call."

"I'm so sorry, Mack. I can't even imagine seeing that, let alone it being your best friend."

Mackenzie nodded, pressing her lips together to keep the rest in. She'd told her therapists over the years what happened, but she'd never admitted to anyone that she wished she'd been the one to die that night. That the world would have been a better place if Mackenzie had died and Jaclyn had lived.

"I'm sorry I asked you about all of this. I didn't mean to upset you."

"You didn't. It... I don't talk about her much. Most people who ask just have some sick fascination with it."

"That's not—"

"I know, Holden. You see things like this all the time. And you're a really good man. That's why I like you."

"I like you, too, Mackenzie." His voice was rough and scraped over all her raw nerves.

Usually when she talked about Jaclyn, Mackenzie felt exposed and vulnerable. On edge. But Holden didn't want to know how she died. He wanted to know how she lived. He wanted to know what kind of person she was, and who Mackenzie was when she knew Jaclyn. And that made Mackenzie remember the good parts about her friend. The things that made Mackenzie come out of her shell and be her true self.

"Jaclyn and I were going to find amazing men to settle down with and demand we buy a townhouse so we could live next door to each other. Or a mansion we could share. It didn't matter as long as we were together. Pete stole so much from me, but I still have my memories of her."

"It sounds like you have a lot of memories of her."

"I do. And the one I held on to the tightest was about the kind of person she knew I could be. Fearless and confident and desirable."

Mackenzie crawled onto Holden's lap. His hands immediately went to her hips. His length hardened between them even as he tried to hold her still. "We don't have to do this."

"I've wanted to feel you inside me since the first night we were trapped. I haven't trusted another man in a long time, so I can't guarantee I'll be any good, but if you're willing—"

"Fuck, yes, I'm willing. You just told me a lot, though. Are you sure?"

Mackenzie closed her eyes and brought Jaclyn's image to her mind. She always felt more confident with her best friend by her side, and this was no exception. "I invited myself back here. I shared my darkest story with you. I am sitting on your lap and asking you to have sex with me. If you aren't interested, please tell me so I can go. If you are—"

Holden yanked her down so fast their teeth clashed. Her lips got caught between them and a tinge of metal hit her tongue. He pulled her body flush with his and thrust up against her, rubbing her clit with his cock.

Mackenzie sighed against him and ran her hands through his hair. Holden was everywhere at once, hands and lips and cock driving her crazy just that fast.

Gone was any last hesitation or fear. All she could think was she didn't want him to stop. Ever.

15

Holden pushed her off the couch, making her panic, then he stood and sealed his lips over hers again. He guided them from the living room, still kissing, to his bedroom. He dropped to his knees just inside the door and kissed her belly.

"I've been dreaming about having you in my bed for months. But now that you're here, I feel like a teenager sneaking a girl into my room and I'm about ready to blow."

"I feel the same," Mackenzie admitted.

"Good, then maybe I'll last longer than you."

She smiled until he licked her belly just above her waistband. He unbuttoned her jeans and eased the zipper down, his tongue following the path. He tugged her jeans until they wiggled over her wide thighs, then pushed them to the floor and licked her through her panties.

"Oh, God."

"Can I taste you, Mackenzie?"

"Yes," she whispered.

"Bed, beautiful."

She turned and found the bed behind her. She laid

down on the edge, her legs hanging over the side of the mattress.

Holden opened a drawer in the nightstand, then closed it. He tossed a strip of condoms onto the bed next to her. "I'm going to enjoy this night."

Mackenzie sucked in a breath. Her core leaked in anticipation. He hooked the sides of her panties and slid them down, one inch at a time and killing her in the process. When they were finally off, he pressed her thighs wide and made himself at home between them.

He blew on her sensitive flesh, and she jumped. One finger eased through her folds, parting them as he stared at her.

Mackenzie wanted to cover herself up. To put her clothes back on and leave, but before she had another thought, he put his mouth on her and she was gone again.

"Oh, fuck."

He licked her clit, then lazily licked around her folds, taking his time capturing all the come that had leaked from her. He pressed her thighs wider with his hands, holding her open to his gaze and his mouth. His tongue delved into her, then he went off like a rocket and sucked hard on her.

"Holden!" The sudden change sent her flying, her body tensing as it tried to release.

He slid a finger into her, the one digit brushing her walls as her body adjusted to the intrusion. It was too much and not enough at the same time. She wanted him, needed him, and was scared of both.

Holden's tongue circled her clit, then swiped over it in rapid succession, the simple move making her head spin and her body remember what it was like to have an orgasm. If anything was like riding a bike, apparently it was riding Holden's face because Mackenzie stopped holding back and shamelessly bucked against his tongue, begging and crying and screaming until she finally came.

She grunted and panted and nearly cried at the relief she felt. But when Holden pushed a second finger into her and kept going, she wasn't sure she'd survive it again.

"Holden. Oh, God. No. Yes. Fuck. Holden!" Her second orgasm barely started before she was screaming her way through it. And when he slowed his pace and extracted his fingers from inside her, she nearly cried at the loss.

It had been a long time since she'd had sex, but it had never been like that.

"Holy fuck," she whispered.

Holden breathed a laugh. "I was almost right there with you."

"I've never done that before. That was... amazing isn't a big enough word."

"I agree."

"You didn't come."

"I tried very hard not to, but watching you is better than anything has ever been. You're beautiful when you come."

"Any chance you're going to let me see what you look like?"

He smirked and reached for one of the condoms he'd tossed on the bed before he blew her mind.

Mackenzie sat up while he undressed. One item at a time hit the floor and made her mouth and her channel water. She wasn't sure where she wanted him more.

"You're gorgeous," she whispered.

He blanched just enough for her to remember how he felt about his looks.

"I didn't mean..."

"I know."

"I don't want you because you're attractive, Holden. But I can't deny I am attracted to you."

He smiled. "That's good. I'm attracted to you, too."

Mackenzie grinned and leaned back as he towered over her. He leaned forward and kissed her, letting her taste herself on his lips. It was new for her, something she'd never experienced before, and turned her on to taste herself on him.

He slid a hand up her thigh and found the wetness seeping from her. He dragged his fingers through it and pumped slowly in and out of her body. She twitched around his finger, ready for him.

Holden leaned back and withdrew his finger, licking it before he tore open the condom wrapper. "Are you comfortable taking off the rest of your clothes?"

Mackenzie looked down and chuckled. "You made me so crazy I forgot I still had them on." She leaned up and pulled her sweater off, then unhooked her bra. Holden took both and tossed them to the floor, then lined himself up at her entrance.

"Are you ready?"

She bit her lip and nodded. "Just go slow."

"I will."

He pressed the tip of his erection against her entrance. Her body tightened, resisting. She wasn't this worried when she had sex for the first time, but back then, it was just something she did. This time, with Holden, it was like her first in a whole new way.

"I'm sorry," she whispered, the emotions tightening her throat.

Holden leaned over her and kissed her softly. He didn't give up on the rhythm as he kissed her.

Mackenzie let herself sink into his kiss. She wrapped her

arms around his neck and kissed him back. He held her legs alongside his hips and, little by little, eased himself into her until he slid past the last bit of her resistance and they moaned together.

"Fucking hell, you feel good," he hissed.

"So do you," she said with a sigh. Her body tingled in all her long-forgotten spots. She hooked her feet behind his back as he withdrew just enough to slide back in.

"I'm sorry this isn't going to last long. I'm going to try to hold out."

"Don't. I'm so beyond good right now. I just want to feel you and watch you."

"Don't blink because it might be over just that fast."

"Holden."

He drew a breath and met her gaze.

"Don't hold back."

His eyes dilated. His cock swelled. And he let loose. His hips pumped like he'd been resisting for far longer than a few minutes. He grunted and shifted, his hips moving and his cock hitting new spots inside her.

She thought she was done, but as he lost himself inside her, he took her with him on a ride she never expected. Her breath caught in her throat, and the look on his face was more determined than ever. Seeing that, seeing him, had her body on fire, ready to make him feel as good as he made her feel.

He thrust, over and over, his movements becoming erratic and his breath rushing out of him in puffs. His eyes were locked on hers, letting Mackenzie see exactly how he felt. He held nothing back, and when he was right there, on the edge of his orgasm, and he couldn't stop it no matter how hard he tried, he slammed deep into her and carried her over the edge with him.

"Holden!" she screeched, the orgasm surprising her as she spiraled into oblivion and never wanted to return to the real world.

Holden collapsed onto her, his sweaty body covering hers, his legs awkwardly hanging off the bed behind them. Mackenzie held onto him, feeling exposed and safe at the same time.

After a minute, he pushed himself up and went to the bathroom. When he returned, he pointed to the door on the opposite side of the room in case she needed to use it.

Mackenzie took a minute to calm herself. The rush of emotions she expected didn't come. It was Holden. He was safe. The anxiety was there, hovering in the back like it was waiting for her to invite it in, but she didn't. She was just good.

Which was a whole new kind of terrifying.

Holden couldn't wipe the smile off his face. Mackenzie was amazing. Not just who she was, how strong she was and how gorgeous she was, but everything about her. And having the honor of not only making her come but being inside her and having her scream his name... Heaven. Holden was in heaven.

He was half-hard and ready again, but Mackenzie was taking a while in the bathroom. Fear started to creep in.

She regretted sleeping with him. She wished they hadn't done anything. She didn't like being vulnerable, but he pushed her.

By the time the door opened and Mackenzie walked out, Holden had talked himself into regretting the night. He had his jeans back on and was reaching for his shirt when Mackenzie caught him.

"Hey," she said timidly.

"Hi." His gaze traveled down her naked form, and fuck him, he wanted her again. Over and over all night long. Just like he said when he tossed the strip of condoms on the bed.

He was such an asshole.

"What's going on?" She wrapped her arms around herself and nibbled on her lip.

"I'm sorry for making you uncomfortable. I did so many things wrong tonight." He pulled his shirt on, knowing he needed to barrier between them or he'd push for more again.

"What are you talking about?"

"I knew it was too soon for you. That you would regret it. I should have held out longer."

"I don't regret it. It looks like you do."

"No," he breathed. "Not even close. But you took a long time in there and I just thought..."

"You should stop thinking, Holden." Mackenzie smiled at him and moved closer. "I expected the anxiety to get to me, but it didn't. I know you who are. I know you're a good person. You've never made me feel like you're manipulating me or trying to control me."

"I wouldn't."

She put her hand on his arm. "I know."

"Do you want me to take you home?" he blurted.

She shook her head slowly. "Not really. Unless you want to be rid of me."

"Not really," he parroted back to her.

She smiled. "Then maybe we can be rid of these clothes you put on."

"Mack, I—"

"I haven't let anyone in for years, Holden. I didn't come here tonight on a whim. I may not have been paying attention to you or hoping you'd notice me for months, but I have been paying attention to you lately. I don't know everything about you, but I feel like I know you. And I like you, Holden. A lot."

He slid his arms around her and held her close. He breathed in the scent of them on her skin, in her hair, and hardened between them.

She smiled against his chest. She kissed her way from one side to the other, the cotton barrier dulling the sensation of her lips and teasing him with the knowledge of what it would feel like to have her body against his again.

"I like you a lot, too, Mackenzie. You have no idea how much."

She laughed softly. "I think I have a little bit of an idea after what we just did."

He breathed her in and held her tight. Her stomach rumbled between them, and he laughed. "Maybe I should feed you again. It sounds like we burned through dinner."

"I'm up for that. But I'd prefer it with a little less on."

He raised an eyebrow and pulled back. "You can have less on than your birthday suit?"

She giggled. "I meant you. You're the one who got dressed."

"That can be remedied." He yanked his shirt off with one hand behind his back, then shoved his pants down, letting his cock spring free. He ached to pull her back down to the bed and devour her again, but she was hungry.

"I still can't believe you wanted me."

Holden stroked himself and nodded. "You shouldn't have any doubts about that right now."

She smiled. "I'm trying hard not to. It's just not normal for me."

"For a man to see how amazing you are? Lucky me they were all so blind."

"You know what I mean. I'm not the ideal woman. My hips are too wide and my body isn't tight or toned. I've fought it my whole life, wishing I looked more like someone like Isabel."

Holden slid his hands over her curves and groaned. Her skin was soft and smooth. The places she saw as not good enough made him want to lick and suck and fuck her all the more. "You're ideal for me. I think you're beautiful, and I'm barely holding myself together to not throw you on the bed and have you again, but you're more than that for me. You're smart and clever and creative. You have compassion for others and you're willing to go out of your way for them. You are a good person. That's more attractive to me than your hips that held me tight when I licked you and your body that rippled with your pleasure as you came. Do you have any idea how sexy it is to watch your orgasm travel through your entire body? To see how you tremble when I hit the right spot? To feel you coming before you do because your body is rolling with the need to let go? That's why I didn't last long tonight. Not because it's been months, even though it has, or because I've been fantasizing about you, even though I have, but because you are so fucking gorgeous when you come that I about lost my damn mind more than once watching you. And I can't wait to see it again and again, any time you're willing to let me lick and suck and fuck you, Mackenzie. Any time."

She sucked in a ragged breath and blew it out slowly. "How about now?"

"Any time, beautiful."

"Holden, please," she whispered, and he didn't make her ask again.

He pushed her onto the bed, not too gently. She bounced once while he sank to his knees. He wasn't going slow this time. He was still going to savor her, but he wasn't going to take his time. He was going to make her scream and tremble and beg him for more until she was so wrung out the only way he knew she was coming was from those ripples her body made when she fought it.

He licked her from bottom to top and sucked hard on her clit. She bucked against him instantly. He slammed a finger inside her, groaning when he felt how stretched out she still was from his cock a few minutes earlier. He added a second finger, and her channel leaked around him, soaking between her legs.

He wanted to stroke himself while he ate her, but he knew he'd come if he did that, so he used his other hand to grab her breasts and feel them bounce as she fucked his face.

It wasn't long before she whimpered and the first of her rolls shook. He set his focus on her clit and flicked it quickly with the very tip of his tongue. He thrust a third finger into her, and she shook. She was right there, on the edge, ready to fall. And he was ready to catch her.

He sucked her clit into his mouth, and she lost her mind. Thrashing and moaning, she came with his name on her lips and her thighs locked around his head. Pure male pride swelled inside him and thudded through his dick. He made her do that. He made her feel that good. Made her body shake like that until it poured out of her.

Holden grabbed one of the condoms that he hadn't stuffed back into his drawer yet. She moaned when he withdrew his hand, and he nearly abandoned the condom to make her come again. She whispered, "Inside me, please," and he went back to his task.

With the condom on, he stood and slammed into her in one move. She gasped and moaned. Her legs wrapped around him as her eyes struggled to open. When she pried them up, a sleepy, satisfied smile lifted her lips.

Holden didn't wait. He retreated, then slammed back into her, watching the way his impact made her body roll. When her flesh settled again, he did it again. She clamped down on him, and he was gone.

He pounded into her, one roll joining with the next until her body bounced with the force of each stroke. She panted and cried out, but she never once asked him to slow or stop. She whispered yes, and he knew she was just as lost as he was.

"Mack, I'm almost there. Are you with me?"

She shook her head. "No. Not yet. That's okay."

It wasn't okay for him. Holden withdrew and dropped to his knees. She groaned in frustration until she felt him between her thighs. He sucked her clit into his mouth and flicked the tightened nub with the tip of his tongue. Almost instantly, she came, screaming and clawing at the sheets before she grabbed the back of his head and shamelessly rode his face through one orgasm and right up into another.

"Inside me. Now. Please, Holden," she begged.

He did as she asked and let himself lose control. He spread her thighs wide and slammed in deeper than before. She writhed against the hold he had on her legs, but the way her body rippled told him she wasn't unhappy about it.

"Oh, God, oh, God, oh, God, yes!" she screamed as she finally came. Her channel locked down on him, making it harder for him to retreat.

He didn't want to, anyway. He slammed in and let go, his

balls pulling up tight as his entire body tingled with his release.

"Mackenzie!" he shouted. Sweat sprouted from every pore on his body and shivers raced through him, making him tremble with aftershocks.

Holden sank to his knees. His head fell onto her belly, and she wove her fingers into his hair. Her stomach rose and fell with each breath she took, lifting his head.

Holden wanted to lay there forever. With Mackenzie in his bed and her hands on him. Nothing could possibly be better than that.

16

———

HOLDEN FINALLY GOT OFF THE FLOOR AND LET MACKENZIE UP off the bed. He pulled her in for a kiss, then squeezed her butt when she walked by to go to the bathroom.

Holden grabbed a pair of sweatpants and left a tee on the bed, in case Mackenzie wanted something more comfortable to wear. He went to the kitchen in search of snacks.

When Mackenzie made it out there, wearing his shirt, Holden grinned and let his gaze trail down over her curvy legs. Legs that were wrapped around his shoulders not long ago. He shifted his growing erection and focused once more on the food.

"Is that a cheese plate?" Mackenzie asked.

"Do you not like cheese? I can get something else."

Mackenzie shook her head. "I love cheese. I just don't usually have a cheese plate in my fridge."

"I bought a few different kinds last time I went to the store. I couldn't pick one, so I grabbed a bunch and cut them up. And they have these thinly sliced meats. It was a total impulse."

"Well worth it," Mackenzie said, picking up a piece of Parmesan. She popped it into her mouth and grinned. "So good."

Holden chose a cube of cheddar jack and stacked it on a cracker. They each tried the different cheeses and meats, some with crackers and some alone, until the entire plate was gone.

"I need to buy cheese more often," Mackenzie said as she sipped a glass of water.

"Or you can just come here and eat mine."

She smiled again. "I like that plan, too."

Holden busied himself cleaning up the kitchen, then turned to face her. "Do you want me to take you home?"

"You can, but I am also enjoying my time with you. If you need time to yourself, though, I get that. I am used to being alone most of the time, and spending too much time with others can get to me."

"Is that how you're feeling?"

She shook her head. "Spending time with you is different for me."

"Me, too."

"So?"

"So, do you want to stay?"

"I think I do. If that's okay."

Holden grinned and circled the island. She tilted her head back to look at him, leaving her neck exposed. He slid his fingertip down the column of her throat. She shivered but didn't pull back. "It's definitely okay for you to stay here. Whenever you want."

"Good."

He kissed her slowly, softly, teasing them both until they were panting. It was still early, and Holden knew they were both going to be sore by the morning if they kept going the way they were.

"Movie?"

"Good plan," Mackenzie said, understanding needing a break.

They barely paid attention to the movie, choosing to tease each other and talk the entire time. When the movie ended, they raced back to the bedroom and drove each other crazy until neither of them could stay awake any longer. The last thing Holden thought of before he fell asleep was how much he hoped she'd be willing to go out again over the weekend. And all the days in between.

DAMON KNEW he was being followed. He even knew it was Trevor. What he didn't know was why the little fucker hadn't made himself known yet. It had been two days. He'd had plenty of chances to kill Damon, or try, but he'd just been watching him.

Damon finally had enough. He was sick of watching his back and wanted to know what the boss thought of his gift.

The car was parked at the back of the lot, in the shadows where Trevor could sit and go unnoticed. Damon could feel his eyes and knew he had to be quick or Trevor would realize something was going on.

Damon slipped out the side door of the convenience store. He kept his gaze on the car. He couldn't see Trevor, but the piss-ant was too dumb to know something was going on. Damon crept along the shadows, waiting for his moment to make his move. If he caught Trevor off-guard, he could find out what the boss wanted and maybe take Trevor out in one night.

What a sweet victory that would be.

Damon made it to the bumper of the vehicle. He wanted to see Trevor's face when he realized he'd been caught. Damon peered around the corner with a grin...

Trevor wasn't in the driver's seat.

"Looking for me?" Trevor asked from right behind Damon.

Damon spun and came face-to-face with the business end of a gun. It wasn't the first time he'd had a gun stuck in his face, and he was going to make damn sure it wasn't the last.

Damon swatted the gun away and swung at Trevor. Trevor ducked, the blow glancing off his shoulder. He swung back, the surprising impact sending Damon into the tailgate.

"Thought you could sneak up on me, old man?"

"Fuck you," Damon spat.

"I'm good. Thanks."

"Why the fuck are you following me?"

"Making sure you don't leave any more gifts for the boss. That didn't go over well."

Damon smirked. "I had no other way to send a message."

"Leaving a knife outside the bedroom? That was your best plan?"

"It worked."

"What worked? You think you did anything other than piss off the boss?"

"That wasn't my plan. My plan was to get to you."

Damon lunged at Trevor, but even with surprise on his side, Trevor avoided him. Damon thought about going for his gun, but he wanted to see the life drain from Trevor's ugly face with his bare hands wrapped around the son-of-a-bitch's neck.

"I guess you don't want to know why the boss sent me," Trevor said, his voice unsteady. Lying.

"To try to kill me. I know how this fucking works."

They chased each other around the vehicle like fucking children, but Damon was getting sick of it. He was there to end a life. And when he was done with that one, he'd move on to Raina. Without Trevor in the picture and with Raina back, the boss would have no choice but to bring Damon back into the fold.

"The boss wants you back," Trevor barked.

The words stopped Damon cold. That was not what he was expecting.

Trevor ducked and peered through the windows at Damon.

Damon glared back. "What does that mean?"

"You can come back."

"As what? Your assistant?"

"As the second," Trevor snarled.

Damon smirked. That was Trevor's position. The spot Damon held before Trevor weaseled his way into power. It was what Damon wanted. It was what he'd been after. Kill Trevor, then Raina, then reclaim his position.

Having it offered to him felt too easy. Nothing was ever so easy with the Company. There had to be a catch.

"Why?"

"What the fuck do you mean, why? You're being handed exactly what you've been wanting. And you're going to fucking question it?"

"Yeah, I am. It's why I'm still alive. It's why my face is the one on the fucking news. I'm seen as the leader. Oh, that's it. The boss knows there's a bounty on my head. If I get picked up, I know where all the bodies are buried. I can sink the Company with a tenth of what I know."

"That may have factored into the decision."

"Yeah? And what else factored in?"

"You never should have left that note."

Damon laughed. It bubbled up like a slow chuckle but erupted into the night air. As he laughed, Trevor grew more and more uncomfortable. Damon knew that note would twist more than a few feathers.

"Shut up," Trevor growled.

"You mean the boss didn't like knowing I stole not one but two whores right out from under your nose? I guess you never volunteered that."

"I don't know why you're still alive. All you've done for years is fuck things up and prove that you're not worth the time invested in you. You—"

"Don't you fucking dare talk to me about value!" Damon bellowed. He got up in Trevor's face, nose-to-nose with the bastard, until Trevor backed up into the side of the vehicle. "I've done more for the Company than twice the men who've gone through those doors. I've kept the secrets and I've buried the bodies and I've done my duty. I'm the one who was smart enough to bring someone on inside the police department. I'm the one who's gotten us out of more murders than you'll ever know were committed. Do you really think there would even be a Company if it weren't for me? Because there wouldn't be. I'm the fucking Company. I'm the one who should be in charge. Because I'm the one who's led us to where we are now. Me. Not you. Not the boss. Me!"

Trevor smirked. He swiped his thumb across his crooked nose. He licked his lips and nodded. "It's nice to know what you really think of your employer. Maybe I should go back to the boss and relay that message."

"You can relay whatever fucking message you want. I'm not coming back after that weak-ass offer."

"Weak-ass offer? It's exactly what you want?"

"No. It's not. Not anymore. Not even fucking close. I want to be the boss. I want to be in charge. When you have that offer, I'll listen. Until then…"

Damon surprised Trevor with a quick punch to his gut. Trevor doubled over, the blow strong enough to break a rib or two. The sound of it made Damon hard. Taking care of Trevor was going to be fun, but repeating the pleasure with Raina might have him blow his load before he finished her off.

Damon swung again, catching Trevor on the chin. He moved just enough for the blow to avoid breaking bones. Before Damon could get in another strike, Trevor kicked him in the balls.

Damon went down instantly. His cock hard and his balls aching, his vision faded on the edges. Vomit rose in his throat. He was vaguely aware of Trevor moving around him to get in the vehicle.

"No wonder that bitch ran out on you. But no worries. That FBI agent protecting her is keeping her real warm at night these days."

Damon tried to call out, but Trevor was gone. Damon collapsed onto the ground, unable to choke back the bile any longer. It landed on his hands and brought up a fresh wave. He heaved, this time not getting anything up.

He crawled to the side and sucked in a breath. Asphalt, snow, and vomit blended in his senses. Fucking Trevor. And fucking Raina. FBI agent? Damon was going to kill them all. One by one. And he was going to enjoy it.

MACKENZIE'S PHONE rang just as she was finishing her shift. She didn't recognize the number, but instead of letting it go to voicemail like she would normally do, she answered.

"Hello?"

"Hello, Mackenzie. This is Francesca. I was hoping we could talk."

"Um, sure." Mackenzie didn't feel right refusing when she'd asked the woman for help, but she was also uneasy about why she'd call.

"I wanted to thank you for all the help you've given us over the last few weeks. I know we wouldn't be where we are without your assistance."

"We really aren't anywhere, it seems. The threat is still out there."

"True, but I believe that will change. I was wondering if you were available tonight. For dinner. I think it's time we all speak. Openly. If you're willing."

Mackenzie was surprised but happy. She hadn't seen Francesca since the day she burst into Braden Wright's home and accused Jessica German of killing a very alive Karli Sloane. Since then, Mackenzie had learned a lot and seen a lot, and she was no longer as convinced that Jessica had anything to do with what happened that day.

"If you have other plans, we can reschedule. Or if you're not interested—"

"I am. Interested. And I don't have other plans. I would like that. Thank you."

"Excellent. Marcus said you should be getting off work around this time, so I'm hoping that means you can come here shortly. Whenever is good for you. I also have someone who would love the chance to meet you and thank you for sharing my name."

Jill. Mackenzie wondered if she'd ever meet the woman. And she wondered how she was doing since she left her boyfriend after he hurt her. "I would like that very much. And yes, I'm done with work. I can head to you now if that's okay."

"Absolutely. I'll see you soon, Mackenzie."

"Bye."

Mackenzie looked at her phone for a minute, then shook her head with a smile. Francesca was a good person to have a connection to. She was looking forward to getting to know her a little better.

Mackenzie parked in the small lot behind Shelter in the Storm. It was only big enough for half a dozen cars, and Mackenzie got the last spot there. She just hoped she didn't take it from a guest.

The house was beautiful on the outside. An older style that was popular many, many decades ago, but it had clearly been updated with the security system that surrounded the property. Mackenzie would bet the windows and doors were also new, and nearly indestructible.

The front door opened as soon as Mackenzie stepped up onto the porch. Francesca smiled warmly and welcomed Mackenzie inside.

"It's freezing out here. I didn't want you to have to wait. We obviously don't leave the door unlocked."

"I understand. And thank you. I parked in the lot behind the house. Is that okay? I don't want to make anyone have to walk and risk getting hurt."

Francesca waved her hand. "You're good. The lot is for staff. Our guests don't have their own vehicles, for safety reasons. If they do, they're not parked here."

"Oh, that makes sense. I didn't think of that."

Francesca led the way through the house toward the back, where she let Mackenzie into a small, packed office.

"I wanted to speak alone for a few minutes before everyone else arrives."

"Oh, um, okay." Mackenzie took the seat Francesca pointed to and folded her hands in her lap. She was nervous, worried about what the older woman was going to say to her.

Francesca smiled warmly. "Don't worry about me, Mackenzie. I just wanted to thank you for sending Jill here. She is still healing, but she'll be okay. She's going to move back home, to be near her family and far away from Rick."

"That's great news. I hate getting calls like hers. Listening when there's nothing I can do. I was happy to hear she was ready to get help."

"Not everyone is. And not everyone trusts that the help is real. But in just a few short weeks, you've shown how good of a person you are. Between Jill and Edie, those women owe you their lives."

Mackenzie shook her head. "I was doing my job with Jill. And Edie... How could I not help her?"

"You'd be surprised how many people aren't willing to help a stranger. And you went above and beyond with Jill. I know Edie is very appreciative of you."

Mackenzie narrowed her eyes. "Have you met Edie?"

Francesca nodded. "I have. She is considering coming here to stay when she gets out of rehab. Her apartment was rented to someone else when she stopped paying rent. All her things were donated or sold. She has nowhere to go."

"She can stay with me."

Francesca smiled kindly. "That decision will be up to Edie. But I will caution you that she might feel safer here.

Where we have security and are under police protection. If she chooses to come here, I don't want it to be something that upsets you."

Mackenzie exhaled slowly. "You're right. I understand that. She needs to feel safe. She's been through too much."

"Yes, she has. And there are more women like her out there. Penny was one of them. These people, these women, Damon has ruined lives. He's been killing people for decades."

"What?"

"We should go into the dining room. The others will be waiting. And we'll tell you everything, Mackenzie. You're one of us."

Mackenzie followed Francesca back down the hallway and into the dining room. The bomb Francesca dropped wasn't something that surprised Mackenzie as much as something that she suspected but had no proof of. The way Francesca said it made it seem like she had proof.

Jessica German, Karli Sloane, and one other woman were in the dining room. Mackenzie thought the woman was at Braden Wright's house that day, but she wasn't positive.

The women were laughing at something Jessica German said. They all stopped when Mackenzie and Francesca walked in.

"Ladies, I believe introductions would be beneficial here. You all know who Mackenzie Chambers is. For a little more detail, Mackenzie has been instrumental in gathering new information that is bringing us closer to finding the sick bastard who's tormented each of us over the years. Macken-zie, you know Jessica German. She's an executive assistant at Birds of a Feather and has been friends with Karli since childhood. Karli Sloane was an art therapist but is now on leave while the threat against her is under investigation. And Stacey Allen is a counselor right here in this building for me."

"Nice to meet you all," Mackenzie said.

They all smiled at her. The room was tense. Them against Mackenzie. She knew they didn't trust her, which made her wonder again why she was there.

Jessica was the first to make a move. She crossed the room to Mackenzie and smiled. "I know when we first spoke, you were seeing history repeat itself. I'm sorry for causing that kind of trauma for you. You wanted to see the right person pay for what happened that day, and I understand that. I sincerely hope that you will one day see that we are all trying to do the same thing. Karli has been my friend forever, and not only would I never hurt her, I'd never hurt anyone."

Mackenzie nodded. "I did some research on you. I didn't want to believe it at first, but I was wrong to accuse you of killing her. You never stopped fighting to find the truth. And you did find the truth. Too bad Damon Street silenced the man who killed Edie's cousin before he could confess."

"He confessed to me. It'll never be public, but he did. He told me what he did. And Tonya wasn't the first woman he killed. He was a sick man, someone the world is better off without, but he got off too easily. That said, I'm not sure he would have ever regretted what he did and he likely would have found a way to kill again, so it's better he's gone."

Mackenzie shivered.

"This is a dark world, Mackenzie. We think we all need to talk, but only if you're ready to be a part of all of this. Are you?" Francesca asked.

"Absolutely."

Francesca looked at the others, and they all took seats at

the table. Mackenzie sat next to Francesca, and the older woman started to tell her story about when she met Damon Street.

When Francesca was done, Stacey talked about a former guest who was killed by her ex-husband, a man who was then killed by Damon.

Mackenzie knew Jessica and Karli's stories, but hearing it all together, knowing the way Damon had infected these women's lives, and the lives of so many others, it made Mackenzie grateful she was no longer looking into him alone.

"What do we do now?" Mackenzie asked.

"Now we find him. And we make him pay for all his crimes. Not just one or two, but all of them. We need him to go away for good," Francesca said.

"I agree. But he's not working alone. There are others," Mackenzie said.

"And eventually, we'll find out who they are. For now, we only know about Damon," Francesca said. She sighed and leaned back in her seat, defeated and frustrated.

"And Trevor," Mackenzie said.

"Trevor?" The other women exchanged a glance. "Who's Trevor?"

"He's the man who held Edie. He was the one who imprisoned her. He's the one who'll go down for what happened to her, not Damon."

"You have a name?" Jessica asked.

Mackenzie nodded. "I assumed you all knew."

They shook their heads slowly.

"Tell us everything," Francesca said.

17

———

Mackenzie shared everything Edie told her. Then she shared all the cases she found that mentioned Trevor. The evidence against him was almost as damning as Damon.

"How did we not know this?" Stacey asked.

"We haven't spoken to Edie much. Just enough to make sure she was okay. I wonder what else she knows," Francesca said.

"I'm not sure you should push her for information right now," Mackenzie said. She didn't want to imagine Edie feeling cornered and scared.

Francesca smiled at Mackenzie. "I agree. And I'm sorry I made it sound the way it did. Edie has told me you've grown close. That you visited her last week and plan to keep going back."

Mackenzie nodded. "After reading about her and knowing a little about what was going on, I was shocked to have her show up like she did. But when she did, I..."

"You felt connected to her. You don't need to explain that to me." Francesca smiled at Mackenzie.

"Thanks. It's more than that, though. She's..." Mackenzie looked around the room at the four women gathered there. Four women who had each other. They were friends. They had each other to lean on. They wouldn't understand what it felt like to be unwanted.

"She's what?" Stacey asked.

Mackenzie drew a breath and focused on Stacey. "Edie was taken because they thought she would go unnoticed. She was one of the unclaimed. That's who Penny was. I get calls from people like that all the time. Who have no one to turn to. But Edie wasn't unclaimed. She had a cousin, and Tonya was in the wrong place at the wrong time." Mackenzie turned to Karli. "I'm sorry. I'm not saying you should have been killed instead—"

"I understand," Karli said with a kind smile. "I've had a hard time accepting another woman died when the killer was after me. Tonya should be here with us, plotting to take down Damon. She should be reunited with her cousin. She should be living her life. She was in the wrong place at the wrong time, and she's not unclaimed either. We remember her, even though none of us ever met her."

"Most people don't remember those who were lost."

"You do, though. You're the one who put the cross on the ground where Penny died, aren't you?" Francesca asked.

Mackenzie hesitated, then nodded.

"I went by there a few days later. Marcus told me about the call. Said you let him know to get the phone she'd used. I wanted to thank her for sharing information so we could help take down the man who killed her. I saw the cross. That was very kind of you."

Mackenzie smiled. "There are lots of people whose deaths go unnoticed."

"And you think you'll be one of them," Stacey said, far too insightful for Mackenzie.

Mackenzie shrugged, unable to force any words out.

"We will notice, Mackenzie," Francesca said, putting her hand on Mackenzie's and squeezing.

"Yes, we will. You're one of us now. A curvy vigilante," Karli said.

"Curvy vigilante?" Mackenzie asked.

Karli handed Mackenzie something small and black. "It's a mask. Frannie used to wear it when she was an exotic dancer."

Mackenzie jerked back and spun to Francesca. Francesca laughed and nodded. "A lifetime ago, yes."

"When she faced Damon, she wore it. It gave her strength. The same strength Stacey got from it when she went to confront Oscar. And Jessica when she found Silver. I wore one when Damon kidnapped my boyfriend. We've all found strength in this unintended sisterhood. We've all faced hell and lived to tell about it. It's not over, but we're fighting to make sure it will be one day. And you're a part of that. You deserve that mask. If you ever face Damon, it'll give you strength."

"Does it have special powers or something?" Mackenzie flipped it over. It looked like a scrap of fabric. Nothing special.

"No special powers," Stacey said. "But when you put it on, you'll feel different. Almost like we're all with you. And if you call us, we will be. You're not alone, Mackenzie. We hope we can all fight Damon together. Take down him and his organization and make our city safer for everyone."

Mackenzie nodded. "Well, I'm not backing down, but I like the idea of not going into this alone."

"Good. Then I think we should all eat. Are you hungry, Mackenzie?"

"Always."

The others chuckled in agreement. Francesca brought in food, and she called for the guests to join them, if they wanted. Francesca introduced Jill and Mackenzie.

Jill sat next to Mackenzie and cried with gratitude. Mackenzie hugged the other woman and told her she was glad she was safe. They ate dinner and talked. All of them. One group. None of them were unwanted or unnoticed. They were strong, but they were definitely stronger together.

Mackenzie left Shelter in the Storm that night with her mask in her hand. She wasn't sure it would bring her the confidence the others said, but she was sure her life had changed that night. For the better.

EDIE LEFT REHAB the following week and went to stay at Shelter in the Storm. Mackenzie visited her over the weekend. Edie did not look okay.

"What's going on?"

Edie shook her head. "I don't know what it is, but I don't think I can stay here."

"Do you want to move in with me?" Mackenzie offered without a second thought.

Edie shook her head. "I appreciate it, but I don't think that would be better. I'm just terrified. This house is old, and it creaks, and every time it does, I jump. Staying with you... I don't think I'm ready to be alone when you're at work. I'm just such a mess."

"No, you aren't. You've been through something most of us will never experience. You aren't a mess. You're doing your damn best."

"But my best is not good enough. I can't sleep, and if I can't sleep, it's all just worse. I don't know what to do."

"Have you tried sleeping pills?"

"No more drugs," Edie said.

Mackenzie shook her head. She felt so insensitive. "I'm sorry. I shouldn't—"

"No, it's fine. Before, I would have taken something without a second thought. But now... I don't know what's safe. Can I take ibuprofen? What about cold medicine? I feel out of control."

"I wonder if you could go to the safe house," Mackenzie said.

"What safe house?"

Mackenzie looked at her friend, a woman she knew was not a double agent, and wondered why no one had offered the option to her. "Damon's ex-girlfriend is being held at a safe house. He's tried to kidnap her more than once. She's under protection from the FBI. I wonder if you could stay with them."

Edie shook her head slowly. "I doubt that would be an option. I'm not important. I got away."

"You will be a witness."

"No, I won't. I was high most of the time. I can barely remember anything that happened. My life isn't valuable."

"Don't say that," Mackenzie snapped. "Never say that. Your life has value. You are a good person. What happened to you was not your fault, and you can't think that it was."

Edie shrugged. "I was an easy target—"

"These people are professionals. You were unlucky. And

you are going to help take them down. Let me see if there's an option."

Mackenzie called Marcus and explained the situation with Edie the best she could. Marcus said he'd noticed she looked tired and didn't seem to be comfortable there. He promised to call back shortly.

"We'll find out soon."

Less than five minutes later, Marcus called back to say Edie could move. If she wanted to.

"It's up to you," Mackenzie told her.

"What if I can't sleep there, either?" Edie whispered.

"Then we'll figure out something else. But until then, you could try it. It's probably smaller, and it's four people, including you."

Edie inhaled and nodded. "Okay. I'll go."

MACKENZIE DIDN'T LIKE NOT BEING able to see Edie regularly, but she was definitely enjoying seeing Holden often. Their work schedules didn't line up all the time, but it was enough that they were able to go out at least once a week.

Mackenzie also started spending time with the curvy vigilantes, as they called themselves. The women were funny and smart and a lot of fun to be around.

Life was good. It was a strange feeling for Mackenzie, but it was. She couldn't remember the last time she felt like herself, and like that was okay. Nights with Holden, days helping people, and time with new friends all made her feel complete.

As long as she didn't think about how quickly December was flying by or that she'd be spending Christmas alone, like she always did.

Mackenzie had worked the last three years on Christmas. It should have been her turn to be off, but she volunteered to work, knowing her coworkers with families would get more out of it. Mackenzie didn't really care. The money was good, and usually it was a quiet day.

The call center was hushed when she walked in that morning, like a library, instead of busy with chatter. Mackenzie didn't mind. There were only three others working with her, one of whom was Eric.

Mackenzie told herself she should be doing more research on Damon and Trevor, but there was something wrong about looking into those two on Christmas. Like the holiday horror movies that seemed to dominate theaters. It just felt extra creepy.

The phone only rang a few times, once for a woman who set fire to her kitchen and once for a couple who ran off the road into a snowbank. Mackenzie sent crews to both calls and knew they would be okay.

She logged out and went to the break room to heat up her lunch. Holden made lasagna a few nights earlier when she'd gone to his house for a date, and he'd insisted she keep the leftovers. As the scent of it filled the break room, she was glad he had.

"Ooh, that smells good. When did you learn to cook?" Eric asked, barging into the break room with a smile.

"Holden cooked it," Mackenzie blurted before she could stop herself.

"You two are still together? No way. I didn't know that."

Mackenzie smiled and nodded, turning back to the microwave and willing it to cook faster so she could take her food back to her desk and eat without an inquisition.

"You two just hit it off after you were trapped together,

didn't you? Isabel was not happy. But between you and me, she's never happy."

Mackenzie smiled over her shoulder at him. She was not looking to get into a conversation with him. Not when she was sure everything she said would get back to Isabel.

"I always thought Holden was a nice guy. I'm happy for you, Mackenzie. You deserve someone good."

"Thanks," she said, softening a little toward Eric. Maybe he wasn't so bad after all.

"I know people here haven't always been welcoming, but I really do hope you'll come out with me sometime. You can meet my husband."

Mackenzie drew a breath and let go of her fears. She'd already let Holden in, and she let the curvy vigilantes in. She could make room for one more friend. She turned to Eric and smiled. "That would be really nice. And thanks."

"Absolutely. You should bring Holden, too. He's so handsome. Don't tell my husband that, though. He's the jealous type. Not that it would matter since you and Holden are so serious. Isabel is going to be so mad when she hears you two are still together. She thought she had her claws in him deep. She kept going on and on about how cute their babies would be."

Eric's comment was a reminder that he was Isabel's friend first. He might not have meant anything by it, but Mackenzie wasn't willing to draw the attention of Isabel. She knew the woman was capable of making her life a living hell.

The microwave beeped, and Mackenzie turned to get her food. She moved it around and cut into the center to make sure it was hot all the way through. "Holden is very cute. It would be hard for any woman to not want him. We're casual, though. I wouldn't expect him to go somewhere just because I asked, you know? We're not like that."

"Ahem."

Mackenzie spun and found Holden standing in the door. He did not look happy.

"Holden," she squeaked.

"Just grabbing a snack." He stomped across the break room to the snack machine. He fished his wallet out of his pocket and snatched a dollar from inside.

Mackenzie gawked at him and turned to Eric, who only smirked as he walked out.

He set her up. The jerk set her up. And she fell right into it.

"Holden," Mackenzie said.

"Don't," he barked. He shoved his wallet and his dollar back into his pocket and slammed out of the break room.

Son of a bitch.

HOLDEN KICKED himself as he walked out of the break room. He thought he'd surprise Mackenzie when he saw her in there. It was the first day the hallway between their areas was open again, and he wanted to see her. Like a Christmas present he hadn't expected. When he walked down the hall and found her in the break room talking to Eric, Holden smiled. Then he heard what she said about him.

Very cute. Casual. We're not like that.

He was such a fool. He thought they were exactly like that. He hadn't spent as many nights with her as possible because he thought they were casual. He thought they were anything but casual.

Guess he was wrong.

Holden was almost back to his side of the building when he heard his name. Against his better judgement, he stopped and waited for her to catch up to him. He crossed his arms and glared at her as she raced toward him, willing his cock not to respond to the way her body bounced as she ran.

Fucking hell, it was just like when she came.

Down, boy.

"Holden, I'm sorry about that. I didn't mean it the way it sounded."

"Really? You didn't mean to tell one of your coworkers that we're barely more than friends?"

"I did, but—"

"Then what did I misunderstand?"

"He was talking about Isabel and how she was going to be mad when she found out we were together, and I just panicked."

"You panicked about my ex? Why?"

"Because she's perfect. She's beautiful, and she matches you, and everyone knows the two of you should be together. When they find out—"

"Whoa. No. First, Isabel and I should not be together. Second, no one gets a vote on that except me. I decide who I want to be with."

"I'm sorry. I just... Eric mentioned her, and I got all twisted up. I should have just let him talk."

"Yeah, you should have. I don't care what he says, but I care a lot about what you say. That wasn't okay, Mackenzie. I wanted to see you today. I was hoping you were working the holiday, too. And instead of being able to ask if you want to get together this weekend, I'm... I don't know. I need to get back to work."

"Holden," she said, reaching out to hold him there.

He looked down at her hand on his arm and back up at her. If he wasn't so angry, he would have wrapped her up and kissed the hell out of her. But she made him feel like he was nothing more than the good-looking guy Isabel thought he was. She made him feel brainless.

"I'm sorry," she whispered.

He nodded and turned to go, letting her hand fall from his arm. He didn't look back.

He pushed through the door into the bay and kept going, up the stairs and into the weight room. He needed to hit something or run or do something to get rid of the anger inside him.

"Well, hello," Isabel said from the corner of the weight room.

Holden barely bit back his groan.

Isabel stood and walked toward him. "I know that look. You're upset about something. Let me guess, new girlfriend troubles?"

"Shut up, Is."

"There's no need for that," Isabel said. She pouted, sticking her breasts out and tilting her head to the side. Once upon a time, he thought the pose was sexy, but now she just looked like a spoiled brat trying to get her way.

"I didn't come here to talk to you."

"No, but you found me anyway. Just like you found me in the bunk room last week, and in the kitchen a few days ago, and—"

"Enough! You make it sound like something happened any of those times. It's a small station. There are only so many places we can go. It stands to reason we'll run into each other sometimes."

Isabel sauntered toward him, shaking her hips and holding his gaze.

Holden raised a brow, wondering what she thought she was going to accomplish.

"You can play house with the fat operator, but one day you'll realize I was right about everything. I was right about us being good together. I was right about smiling and getting your way. And I'm guessing, since you haven't left, you already know I was right about being a flight paramedic. I'll be waiting when you come crawling back to me and want a good fuck. But don't wait too long because I don't suck dick for too many men. And never for ones who don't know exactly what they have right here." She waved her hand over her body. She rubbed against him as she walked by.

Holden wanted to back away from her, but he wasn't going to let her win.

She stalked out of the weight room, and a minute later, a door closed down the hall.

Holden let out the breath he was holding. He walked to the punching bag in the corner and slammed his fist into it. The speed bag slammed against the platform and bounced back. Holden knew he should wear gloves, but the feel of the vinyl against his knuckles was the wake-up call he needed.

After a few good hits, Holden walked away with the bag still swinging. He was out of breath and pissed off, but he knew what he had to do. Stop fucking around and get his life in line.

He spent too much time doing what others wanted him to do. Too much time listening to his mother or his father or his girlfriends or friends. Too much time ignoring what he wanted, and who he wanted.

He was done.

Holden knocked on the door to the supervisor's office

and waited for McCall to wave Holden inside.

"What can I do for you?"

"I want to become a flight paramedic," Holden blurted.

McCall nodded, not giving anything away. "Is this your way of putting in notice?"

"What? No, sir. I have been thinking about it for a while, but I haven't figured it out. I love what I do, but I..."

"Want a new challenge. I understand that. There's nothing wrong with that. Have you looked into training? I'm not sure when the next class starts."

Holden shook his head. "I haven't done anything. I've only told two people, and one wasn't very supportive. It's made me question if I can do it or not."

"First, don't let other's opinions mold your mind. Figure out what you want and go after it. Second, I have a friend who's a flight paramedic. Let me give him a call and I'll get some information for you. We'll go from there."

Holden nodded. "Thank you, sir."

"You're welcome." He stared at Holden for another moment. "Is there something else?"

Holden shook his head. "No, sir. Thank you for not laughing at me."

"Never. You're good at what you do. They'll be lucky to have you if that's what you decide is your next move."

"Thank you, sir."

Holden left the office and exhaled a breath. He had a lot of respect for McCall. The man had been a paramedic for decades and he was a respected and fair supervisor. Holden enjoyed working for him and trusted his opinion. Knowing McCall believed in him gave Holden the reassurance he needed to go after that dream.

It also gave him to confidence to go after his other dream. Holden went back down the newly rebuilt hall to the other side of the building. He pushed his way into the break room and pulled out his phone to text Mackenzie.

> I'm sorry. I was a jerk, and I had no reason to react that way.

He watched as she picked up her phone and read his text. A minute later, a response popped up on his phone.

> It's my fault. I should have known better when Eric started asking me questions. We've never been friends, and there was no reason to think he wanted to be now. I'm sorry I hurt you.

> It's okay. Any chance you want to make it up to me?

> I'm not having sex in a closet.

> LOL! Not what I was thinking. But maybe you could come to the break room.

She spun in her chair and saw him watching her. She was up and moving toward him in a second, and when she burst into the break room, she stopped.

"I am sorry."

"I know. I am, too. After I left here, I saw Isabel. It reminded me that I need to live my own life. Not someone else's. I let my old fears get to me. I know that wasn't you."

"Do you forgive me?"

"There's nothing to forgive, but I do want to tell you something."

"What's that?"

"I asked McCall about flight paramedic training. He's going to reach out to a friend."

"That's awesome! Congratulations, Holden."

"Thanks. Think you might be willing to celebrate with me tonight?"

Mackenzie smiled and finally moved across the break room to him. She wrapped her arms around his neck and looked up into his eyes. "Absolutely."

18

―――――

DAMON WAITED OUTSIDE OFFICER BERNARD'S HOUSE IN THE darkness. A call to the department said the officer was off duty an hour ago, so Damon staked out the place. It was a risk, but he was out of options. The asshole owed him, and Damon was ready to collect the debt.

A car pulled into the driveway, lights shining on the house and narrowly missing Damon's hiding place. He needed to catch Bernard off-guard if he was going to get any information out of him.

Bernard got out of the car and grabbed a small duffle bag from the backseat. He walked up the three steps to his porch and unlocked the door. He went inside and the click of the door locking behind him made Damon smile.

Bernard had no clue he was there.

Damon had already been inside the man's house. Had already left a window unlocked so he could sneak back in after the other man went to sleep. All he had to do now was wait.

The night darkened and lights in the houses all around him went out. Damon stared at Bernard's house, not wanting to miss a thing. When the lights downstairs went out, lights upstairs went on. It was almost time.

Damon inched closer to the house and watched the upstairs windows. The last light went out, and Damon smiled. He was that much closer to the answers he needed, and the revenge he craved.

He was a patient man, and he knew the longer he waited, the better things would go. An hour passed before Damon made his move, opening the window he'd accessed earlier and slipping inside without a sound. He listened to the house once he was in, confident Bernard was asleep.

Damon crept up the stairs and to the bedroom he'd seen lights on earlier. The door was open, giving Damon a view of the man asleep in the room. Damon walked over to his bed and pressed his gun to Bernard's temple.

Bernard jumped, screaming like the fucking pussy he was, and reached for something on his nightstand.

Damon was ready for him and knocked the man's hand away. He pulled the trigger on his gun, a soft pop unheard by the neighbors sleeping just a few feet away.

"What do you want?" Bernard asked. His voice trembled. The scent of fear filled the air.

Damon grinned. "Information."

"Damon?" Bernard barked.

"You owe me," Damon snarled back.

"I don't owe you anything. What the fuck do you think you're doing in my house?" Bernard made a move to get up, but Damon pushed the gun into the center of the man's chest.

"Handcuffs."

"What?"

"Where are they?"

"Fuck you."

Damon aimed at the man's knee and squeezed the trigger. He would have preferred to use his fists, but he knew Bernard could get away before Damon incapacitated him. The gun evened the playing field.

"Ow! God dammit! What the fuck is wrong with you?" Bernard grabbed his knee.

"Where are the handcuffs?"

Bernard scowled in the moonlit bedroom and yanked open the nightstand drawer. He pulled out a pair of handcuffs and held them up.

"I figured they'd have red fur," Damon taunted.

"Fuck you."

Damon snatched the cuffs and grabbed Bernard's arm. He dragged it up to the headboard and snapped the cuffs on, making sure Bernard couldn't get away.

"What in the hell are you doing?"

"Gathering information. I know Raina's being guarded by an FBI agent. Who and where?"

"How the fuck do I know?"

"Because you're a police officer. And you are on my payroll to know these things. So you better start talking."

"You haven't paid me in weeks, and I don't know anything. The captain has been keeping everything hushed. He knows someone is working for you and he isn't letting anyone in unless he knows he can trust them."

"Your job was to be trusted. To be in that circle. If you want a chance to go back and do your job, you need to think real hard about what you saw and heard."

Bernard was quiet for a minute. He closed his eyes and tilted his head.

Damon wasn't interested in his bullshit. He took the butt of the gun and slammed it down on the man's bullet wound.

Bernard screamed and tried to pull his leg away.

Damon took advantage of his distraction and slammed his fist into Bernard's ribs. They didn't crack, unfortunately, but the man immediately tried to double over, held back by the cuffs on his wrist.

"Jesus, fuck!" Bernard spat. He coughed and wheezed and winced with the pain. "How the fuck am I supposed to tell you anything if you do that?"

"Talk fast," Damon growled.

"Okay, fine. I don't know if it matters, but Captain has been meeting with that group. Those military guys. F-BOMB or something. One of them has been there a few times. Blond, quiet, young. The first time he came, there was another guy with him. Someone who looked a lot like him. Maybe a relative. I heard someone say something about him being FBI. He's probably the one keeping your woman warm at night."

Damon slapped the smirk off Bernard's face with the back of his gun. A tooth went flying across the bed.

"I'm gonna fucking kill you," Bernard hissed.

"What else do you know?"

"That's it. The blond is probably the one keeping them in contact. If you follow him, you'll find your bitch."

Damon knew the group Bernard was talking about. They'd kept their noses out of his business, so he kept his nose out of theirs. They'd taken out one of the Company's competitors, and the enemy of my enemy and all that made Damon appreciate them. But if they were helping hide Raina, they were now his enemy.

Damon turned to walk away, but Bernard called out.

"What the fuck? Let me go?"

Damon stopped at the door and looked at the man. He would kill Damon the next chance he had. And he wouldn't think twice about turning on him. Bernard had already drugged Damon once and made him look like a fool. Breaking into the man's home and torturing him put a new target on Damon's back. One he was happy to erase.

He lifted the gun and pointed it at Bernard. Damon pulled the trigger before Bernard had a chance to protest. His eyes went wide as the blood pumped out of the hole in his chest.

Damon smirked, closed the bedroom door, and left the house the way he came in.

"How was your fly-along today?" Mackenzie asked.

Holden grinned. He still couldn't believe McCall got him in with a crew so quickly. Only a week had passed since he'd asked about it, and Holden had already been on two shifts with them.

"It was amazing," Holden said, a smile lifting his lips. He couldn't contain his excitement. "Exhilarating."

Mackenzie grinned back at him. "Good. Have you decided if you're going to go through the training?"

"I think I am."

"You think? What's holding you back?"

He rubbed the back of his neck and looked up at her. She was the only thing Holden had found yet that brought him a bigger boost than saving a life. They'd been dating for a month, but he knew long before then that he loved her. A new job, one with even more unpredictable hours, where he was on call a lot, was going to make their new relationship more of a challenge.

"Talk to me. What is it?"

"I don't want it to come between us."

"What? What are you talking about?"

Holden took her hands and led her to the couch. They could finish cleaning up dinner later. He needed to touch her and talk to her before he lost his nerve. "I can't afford to quit my current job and train for the new one. It's going to mean a lot of hours and months of training. I'm not sure how much free time I'm going to have. And I don't want to do something that'll push you away."

"You're going after your dream. How could I stand in the way of that?"

"I know you wouldn't, but I don't want to lose one dream when I'm chasing another."

"You're not going to lose me," she whispered. Mackenzie looked up at him and adjusted her glasses. She blinked and smiled, but he saw the tear in the corner of her eye.

"What's wrong?"

"What dream are you worried about losing?"

"A future with you." Holden was done holding back.

"We've never talked about that."

"I didn't want to scare you off."

"I'm... Okay, yeah, I get that."

Holden chuckled with her.

"I've spent a lot of years wishing things were different. A lot of years wishing I'd been the one to die that night instead of Jaclyn. I still don't know why he didn't kill me. I always assumed it was so he had someone to pin her murder on, but I don't know if that's the whole truth. Having someone who cares what happens to me is new. It's going to take some getting used to."

Holden pulled her into his arms and held her against his pounding heart. "You might never know why he didn't kill you, but I'm glad he didn't. I'm glad you are here for me to love."

"Love?"

Holden nodded and pulled back just enough to meet her gaze. He smiled and said, "I love you, Mackenzie. You might not be ready to hear it, and I'm sure you're not ready to say it, but I wanted you to know."

She smiled. A single tear rolled down her cheek. "Thank you, Holden."

He lowered his head, giving her time to pull back, but she didn't, and he kissed her. He wanted to show her how he felt, to let her know he was always going to be there for her.

Mackenzie sighed, her entire body relaxing against his. He kept his hands in safe zones, not wanting her to feel pressured to do anything after his confession.

She twisted her body and crawled on top of him, breaking their kiss only to position herself on his lap. Her core was warm and welcoming, and he resisted the urge to rock against her. It wasn't just about sex for him. There was so much more to Mackenzie.

Her hands went into his hair, and she shifted her hips. His cock hardened, anxious to get in on the action, but he ignored it. Until she slid from his lap.

"Mackenzie," he hissed.

She looked up at him through those big glasses of hers and smirked. Dear God, his woman smirked at him. She tugged at the sides of his sweats until he lifted his hips and helped her shove them down. As soon as his cock was free, she abandoned the sweats to wrap a hand around him.

"I've been wanting to do this," she confessed, her gaze focused on his dick. "I'm dying to know how you taste."

She licked one side of his cock, and he jerked against her. It felt so fucking good. Too good. She was going to have him exploding in no time.

"Mackenzie."

"Please let me," she said, imploring him with those irresistible eyes.

Holden sucked in a breath and nodded once.

Mackenzie took off her glasses and set them on the coffee table behind her, then lowered her mouth to his cock. She took him inside, and his eyes rolled back in his head.

"Oh, fuck, Mack."

She hummed, sending a jolt through him to his balls. Lightning exploded behind his eyes. He gritted his teeth and squeezed his hands into fists to stop himself from coming without warning her.

Mackenzie slid her mouth up and down his shaft, licking and sucking. It wasn't polished or perfect, but it was the woman he loved, so Holden enjoyed the fuck out of it. Watching her head bob between his legs, seeing his dick disappear into her mouth, it was better than just about anything else in the world.

She released him and looked up. Her lips were red and her cheeks flushed. If he wasn't mistaken, sucking him was turning her on. Which turned him on even more.

"Tell me if I'm doing something wrong."

"You're fucking perfect," Holden hissed. He hauled her in to kiss her, fucking her mouth with his tongue. She moaned in reply and let herself get lost in the kiss with him. His cock twitched between them, and she pulled back.

Her gaze dropped to the selfish appendage, and she smiled before she sucked him back into her mouth. Up and down, her head moved, driving him closer to the brink than she knew. Holden didn't want to come in her mouth, though, and when he was almost unable to stop, he gently pushed her off him.

"What did you do that for?" she asked, wiping her mouth on the back of her hand.

"I need to be inside you, Mackenzie. I want to feel your pussy around me when I come."

Her eyes widened at the dirty word, but she didn't protest.

"Take off your clothes."

Mackenzie did as he instructed, her body right in front of him to touch as she exposed her skin to him. Holden shoved his sweats the rest of the way off and kicked them to the side, then yanked his shirt off. When they were both naked, he stretched out on the couch and pulled her toward him.

"What are you doing?"

"Sit on my face. I need to taste you."

Mackenzie flushed from head to toe, then climbed on him.

She was soaked before his first lick. He sucked her clit, then fucked her with his tongue, then went back to her clit. She rode his face without shame until she leaned over the arm of the couch and let go.

Holden scooted out from beneath her and grabbed a condom from the side table. He rolled it on while she panted and tried to recover. He positioned himself behind her, kneeling on the couch, and pushed at her entrance.

"Oh, yes," she moaned. She dipped lower, lifting her hips for him.

He pushed inside slowly, dragging it out as long as he could stand. He wasn't going to last long after the way she sucked him and the way she fucked his face, but he wanted to make sure she was satisfied.

Holden reached around her hip and slid his hand down her plush belly. He teased down through the hair between her legs and found her plump clit. He rubbed tender circles around it while he slowly fucked her from behind.

"Holden," she whimpered.

"Yes, beautiful?"

"Please, Holden. I need you."

"I'm right here. I'm not going anywhere."

She whimpered again, and he increased his pace just barely. Her breath hitched, and her core tightened, and his control slipped.

"So good," she whispered.

He tightened the circles around her clit to brush over the sensitive bundle of nerves. She bucked against his hand and thrust her hips back when he pressed in. The change sent a bolt through him, and his control slipped farther away.

"Please," she whispered, and that was the end of his control.

One hand held her hip in place while the other rubbed furiously over her clit. He pounded into her from behind, feeling her body tighten around him as she raced him toward their orgasms.

"Holden," she groaned.

He shifted, and she splintered. She screamed his name. He lost his fucking mind, slamming harder and harder until he thought he was going to explode.

Stars and fireworks exploded behind his eyes. He roared as his orgasm charged out of him, taking every last piece of his soul and depositing it inside her.

He belonged to Mackenzie.

He wrapped his arms around her and prayed that one day she would feel the same. He was hers, and he wanted her to be his. He'd never force it, but he was hopeful. He'd never experienced the kind of connection he had with her, and he knew it couldn't possibly be one-sided.

Holden finally climbed off the couch and let Mackenzie up. It was a becoming a trend for him to collapse on top of her. She smiled and kissed him before she headed for the bathroom. He trashed the condom and collapsed on the couch again, not bothering with clothes.

Mackenzie came back out and smiled when she saw he hadn't bothered to get dressed. She curled up next to him and kissed his chest. "Thank you."

He kissed the top of her head. "Thank you. If you give me a few minutes, we can do that again. Or later. Are you staying tonight?"

She nodded and burrowed in closer. "If that's okay."

"Always."

"I'm going to see Edie tomorrow, though, so I need to go home after lunch."

"It's been a while since you've seen her."

Mackenzie nodded. "I miss her. Is that weird?"

Holden shook his head. "No. Just proves what kind of person you are. Dinner tomorrow?"

"I should be back by then."

"Perfect."

Mackenzie snuggled closer again, and Holden covered them with a blanket.

Maybe she didn't say the words, but having her body tucked against his, their scent of sex on their skin, it definitely felt like love to Holden. He could wait for when she was ready to say it.

DAMON'S PATIENCE was finally going to pay off. He watched the blond guy for six days before the man got in his vehicle and drove out to the edge of town. The house was small, in a quiet area, and the perfect hiding spot for someone trying not to be noticed.

Once the blond man was inside, Damon drove by. He didn't want any of them to know he was there. And he didn't want to take on an extra man. If the research he'd done was correct, the FBI agent that looked like the blond man was his cousin, and the guy's partner was a woman. Damon could handle one man and one woman. Easy.

He went to a convenience store down the street and waited for the second man to leave. He figured if he gave them an hour, he'd be good to go.

Damon left the car he stole behind the convenience store. Someone would find it eventually, but by then Damon would have Raina and he'd be long gone.

He kept off the road, wanting as few people to see him as possible. There was no way of knowing if there were scouts around the place. Better to be silent and invisible.

The house came into view. The vehicle the blond man arrived in was gone. The attached garage likely had another vehicle, maybe two.

Damon would prefer to surprise them after night fell, but he wasn't willing to wait any longer to see Raina. He was hard just thinking about holding her down and forcing himself on her. The fucking bitch deserved to be bloody and bruised when he did it, too. He was getting excited just thinking about it.

Damon crept to the house, watching for cameras and motion detectors as he moved across the small yard. The curtains blocked his view inside the house, but it didn't matter. He was going in, and he was going to get his revenge.

The back door was the best entry point, since it was away from the street. As Damon moved closer, he noticed an egress window into the basement. One that had no cameras and no wires. He smiled and moved toward it.

The window slid open, a soft creak making Damon

pause. When no footsteps hurried toward him, he eased it the rest of the way and stepped inside. The basement was dark and full of stuff, but there was a clear path to the stairs. Damon closed the window and moved across the house.

Voices met his ears when he reached the bottom of the stairs. Chatter. Nothing important. Definitely nothing that said they knew he was there.

One male voice and two... no, three female voices. Damon grinned. Trevor didn't steal Edie back. She was there. Under the same protection. Damon's day was getting better and better.

He crept up the stairs, listening for the voices and trying to pinpoint locations. The man hummed, silverware scratching against dishes. He was in the kitchen. But knives were no match for guns.

Damon carefully twisted the doorknob and pushed the door open silently, just a crack. Damon couldn't see much, but he could see the man. He was about six feet away, with his back to Damon. He was tall but not overly wide. Damon was sure he could overpower the man.

Damon opened the door wider and moved out of the basement. He crept up behind the man, the floor creaking when he was a foot away.

The man turned, his eyes widening for a second as Damon rose his gun and slammed it down onto the man's head. He fell instantly, but the sound of the butter knife he was holding clattering to the floor drew footsteps.

Damon looked up and smiled at the three women. "Hello, Raina."

19

———

Mackenzie double checked the address she was given for the safe house and parked her car. She was excited to see Edie. It had been two weeks, and Mackenzie hoped her friend was doing better. Being somewhere safe and knowing she wasn't alone would help. So would time, but until enough time passed that Edie wasn't terrified with every breath, she needed to feel safe.

Mackenzie got out of her car and closed the door. She grabbed the bag of books she'd picked up at the used bookstore for Edie, and Raina if she wanted to read, too.

Mackenzie locked her car and walked to the door. She knew they would see her coming through the doorbell camera and smiled. She was almost there.

A scream came from inside. Mackenzie stopped. Her breath froze inside her lungs. She looked up at the house, but all the curtains were drawn.

There was another sound inside, like something fell over, and she ran. Her hand wrapped around the mace she carried in her purse, just in case. The bag of books was in one hand, mace in the other. She shifted the books to cradle them and knocked on the door.

Silence echoed back at her.

Mackenzie knocked again, pounding with the side of her fist until it ached from the impact. She'd about given up when the door swung open and the man who haunted the city smiled down at her.

"Welcome to the party, Mackenzie Chambers. It's so nice you could join us."

Mackenzie looked past him to where Edie was bound to a chair. Tears streamed down her face, over the duct tape that covered her lips. Everything inside Mackenzie told her to turn around and run, but she couldn't. She couldn't leave her friend, or the others, at the mercy of the merciless man in front of her.

Damon smiled when Mackenzie took a step toward him. He closed the door behind her and locked it, only then revealing Raina on her knees next to him.

"What did you do to her?" Mackenzie gasped.

Raina's light brown hair was wound tight in his fist. Her lip was bleeding, and the way she was hunched to the side, Mackenzie guessed she had more injuries beneath her clothes.

"Don't worry about her. You're here to see your friend. Edie promised to behave, though. She knows what happens when she doesn't."

Edie whimpered and more tears streamed down her cheeks.

Mackenzie knew there were supposed to be two FBI agents with them. She looked around the room, gasping when she saw a man on the floor in the kitchen.

Damon followed her gaze and smiled. "He didn't put up much of a fight. Shame, though. I was going to have fun taking him down. I'll get to him soon. I had to make sure you were comfortable first."

"I'm not getting comfortable. I'm going to kill you."

A laugh bubbled up from Damon. It started small, then grew little-by-little. He stared at Mackenzie, laughing harder every time he looked at her until he nearly doubled over with laughter.

"Thank you for that. I needed a laugh. It's been a long few weeks. But I have Raina back, so it's all going to be okay now."

"You're not taking her anywhere."

"And you really think you're going to stop me?" Damon moved toward Mackenzie, dragging Raina with him. Raina whimpered and reached up to grab her hair. Damon slapped her hand away and grabbed her chin. Raina cried out. "I told you to stop fighting me. Did you really think you could hide from me? You could shack up with that blowhard and I wouldn't find out. He's not even half the man I am."

"He's three times the man you've ever hoped to be," Raina snarled at him.

Damon tugged her hair, dragging her across the room. He lifted her, using mostly her hair, and tossed her onto the couch. "Don't move."

Raina glared at him, but she didn't make a move.

"What do you think you're going to accomplish here?" Mackenzie asked. Her training taught her to keep them talking. Victim, perpetrator, didn't matter. Just keep them talking. Distract them and find a solution. Her life had never depended on her skills before, but the lives of others did.

None had ever been more important than the people in the house with her right now. Even if she didn't know all of them.

Damon ignored Mackenzie and walked into the kitchen.

He yanked the plug for the toaster out of the wall and sliced through the cord. Then he wrapped it around the man's hands and tied a tight knot. Mackenzie could see his skin turning white beneath the cord, cutting off the blood flow to his hands.

"That's too tight. That's not good for his hands," Mackenzie argued.

Damon snorted. "He's not going to need his hands when he's dead."

Raina squeaked, and Edie sobbed. Mackenzie trembled inside, but she refused to let the monster see her fear.

"Tough one, huh? The other tough one is nursing a killer headache in the bathroom."

"What?"

Damon smirked, and Mackenzie swore the devil himself was looking at her. "You can go see, but she's not going anywhere."

Mackenzie turned toward where Damon indicated and found a blood trail to a closed door. She opened it to a Black woman passed out in the bathtub. Blood oozed into her hair from a cut near her temple. Her chest rose and fell, so she was alive, but she was definitely unconscious. And tied up. Her hands were behind her back and her feet tied together.

Terror swept through Mackenzie. The two people who were supposed to protect Raina and Edie were knocked out. Bound and unconscious. Edie herself was not going to be any help. And Raina...

Mackenzie knew Raina would rather die than be with Damon again, but she also knew Raina would sacrifice herself for others. If Damon threatened to kill any of the people in the house, Raina was likely to use herself as a bargaining chip.

But Damon wouldn't agree to something like that. Not

honestly. He would tell her that, and then kill the rest of them, anyway.

There was no way they were getting out of there alive. Not unless Mackenzie could come up with a way to stop Damon, or notify the police. Too bad one of the requirements of going to the safe house was to turn her phone off and leave it in her car.

Which meant she only had herself to rely on. No one was coming, and no one was going to save them. She was getting the chance she'd been hoping to have for weeks. A little more face-to-face than she'd wished for, but she was getting a chance to bring justice to Damon Street. Justice for Tonya. Justice for Penny. Justice for Edie and Raina. And justice for all the other women Damon had hurt over the years.

Mackenzie might not survive the night, but she was going to make sure Damon didn't get away with one more murder. Even if it was hers.

Mackenzie started to leave the bathroom when the light caught on something tucked under a washcloth on the edge of the sink.

A razor blade.

Mackenzie grabbed the blade and held it in her palm. She was just as likely to cut herself as Damon, but she felt better with some kind of a weapon.

She closed the door and turned back to the living room. Damon was watching her. The sneer on his face was enough to make Mackenzie's skin crawl. She thought about being with Holden. Safe and loved in his arms. She didn't tell him she loved him because the idea of it scared her, but looking at the man who was going to kill her, she knew the fear of Holden rejecting her one day was nothing compared to what she felt at that moment.

If she could go back and tell Holden how she felt, she would in a heartbeat. But all she could do was push forward and hope she had a chance to say the words to him one day.

"Why don't you come and sit with us, Mackenzie Chambers? Get to know us a little better."

Mackenzie swallowed her fear and moved toward the man. Edie watched her carefully, the terror in her gaze enough to almost make Mackenzie break down. But she couldn't. She had to figure out how to control the situation and save them all.

Mackenzie stood near the door, and Damon snickered.

"Are you going to make a run for it, Mackenzie Chambers? Are you going to leave your friends behind?"

"I just don't want to be any closer to you than I have to be."

Damon laughed like she was making a joke. "You never should have come here, Mackenzie Chambers. You should have just stayed behind your call center desk and put your stakes in the ground and believed you were helping people. You never should have come back out into the world."

The breath fled from Mackenzie. She hadn't told many people about the things she'd done. No one knew about the crosses except Francesca and the curvy vigilantes. There was no way they told Damon, which only left one option. He was following her.

"What do you want from me?"

"From you? Nothing, really. You're inconsequential to my plans. The only reason you're still alive is because I'm enjoying you. Not as much as I enjoy Raina, but enough. I heard you were the one who talked to Penny. She was a crafty bitch."

"Shut up," Mackenzie hissed.

"Did you like Penny? Oh, wait. You marked where she

died with a cross, didn't you? She must have left a mark on you."

"She didn't deserve to die."

"How the fuck would you know?" Damon barked, racing toward her. He got up in her face and his stench nearly sent her to her knees. Like he hadn't showered in days and hadn't brushed his teeth in weeks.

Mackenzie breathed through her mouth to avoid throwing up. "Why do you hurt women? You drug them up so they can't fight back and then you beat them and kill them. Is that the only way you get off? You need a woman who won't run away from you?"

Damon backhanded her, sending her to her knees.

He grabbed her hair before she had a chance to suck in a breath and fight back the pain. She looked up at him from the floor, her eyes watering with the pain and her vision blurry. Her glasses were gone. Her cheek burned from the hit. But she wasn't stopping now. She still had the razor blade.

"You don't know one goddam thing about me, bitch."

"I know you only want Raina because she embarrassed you. You hurt her, and she left, and it damaged your fragile fucking pride. You're not a real man. A real man isn't going to hurt a woman. A real man is going to treat her like a fucking queen."

"Is that what Mr. Cross does? He treats you like a queen when he's fucking you until you scream his name?" Damon hissed in her ear.

Bile rose in her throat. She was not going to let him get to her. He didn't know anything about her and Holden. Holden wouldn't betray her, and Damon just made a lucky guess.

"Please, tell me more about how a man should treat a

woman. I'd like to know." He shoved her away from himself and stalked across the room. He took a seat next to Raina, draping his arm around the back of the couch where she was sitting.

Raina started to move away from him, but Damon grabbed her hair and yanked her back to his side. One hand went between her clenched thighs and the other stayed in her hair, controlling her.

"Tell me, Mackenzie Chambers, what Raina wants me to do right now."

"She wants you to let her go," Mackenzie growled at him. She pushed herself back to her feet, keeping the razor blade tucked in her palm. The corner cut into her skin, but she wasn't going to think about that.

Damon barked a laugh and squeezed Raina's leg so hard she winced. "That's not going to happen. Not until I'm done with her. Then I'll leave her body somewhere the cops will find. I'm not a cruel bastard. I don't hide bodies. I like to give the families closure. Make sure someone knows their loved one is dead. I like people to appreciate my handiwork."

"You're a sick son-of-a-bitch," Mackenzie breathed.

"No, I'm not. I'm a man who knows who he is. I've never lied. I've never manipulated. I'm honest."

"Liar," Raina breathed.

"What?" Damon barked, yanking her head back.

"I said you're a liar. I never would have dated you if I'd known who you were. I wouldn't have had anything to do with you."

"You couldn't resist me. All you saw was I had money, and I was willing to spend it on you. You're the cheap kind of whore. No drugs were needed to get you into my bed. Or to keep you there. You just wanted nice dinners and fancy clothes and to be taken care of. And I would have taken care of you, Raina. I would have given you anything you wanted. But you had to start getting nosy. You mouthed off to me and you asked questions. That wasn't okay."

"You had dangerous people in our apartment."

"My apartment," Damon corrected. "I paid for it. I paid for everything. If I pay, I get to decide what happens there. Including what happens to you because I paid for every-fucking-thing you had."

Raina cowered from him as he yelled in her face. She swallowed audibly.

Mackenzie glanced at Edie, but Edie looked borderline catatonic. She was beyond her fear now, into a place where she simply existed outside of her body.

"And you think that's a fair arrangement?" Mackenzie asked, bringing Damon's attention back to her.

Damon turned his head slowly to look at her. "Yes, I do. If Raina hadn't started poking around where her nose didn't belong, she never would have had anything to worry about. For the rest of her life."

"I'm surprised by that because it seems as though you're having some trouble right now. No shower, no bathroom. You're what? Living in a car? Maybe on the side of the road. Kind of cold for that. I'm guessing being a wanted man makes it hard to run your business. Move drugs and money and women. People probably don't want to have much of anything to do with someone the entire county is looking for. What would have happened to Raina if she were still with you? Would she have just gone along with it all?"

"If Raina were still with me, none of this would have happened!" Damon jumped off the couch and rushed over to Mackenzie. He got in her face. His eyes were wild with anger.

This was Mackenzie's one chance to get the upper hand

on him. She flipped the blade in her hand, grasping the blunt edge between her thumb and fingers, and sliced it across his face.

HOLDEN WAS STARING into his fridge, trying to plan dinner for his date with Mackenzie, when his phone rang. He closed the fridge and jogged to the living room where he left it.

He debated letting it go to voicemail, but the local number had him swiping to answer it.

"Hello?"

"Mr. Cross, this is Captain Marcus Patrick. Do you have a minute?"

"Yes, sir. What can I do for you?"

"I was wondering if Mackenzie Chambers is with you. I apologize for reaching out, but we were supposed to meet thirty minutes ago and I haven't heard from her."

Holden checked the time on his phone. "I don't know. We have plans tonight, but she was supposed to go see Edie this afternoon."

"What time?" Marcus asked.

"Over an hour ago. She could have lost track of time, but—"

"But she could also be in trouble," Captain Patrick finished for him. "I've tried calling her, but her phone has been going straight to voicemail, so it must be off. I know she was told it had to be off going out there, but she's never missed a meeting we've scheduled."

"I didn't have a good feeling about her going. I know this is a lot to ask, sir, but I'd like to go with you. I'm assuming you're going out there."

"I am," Captain Patrick said hesitantly.

"Please, sir, I know you don't know me, but all I care about is making sure she's safe. I'm a paramedic, and if there's anything going on..." Holden couldn't bring himself to say the rest. He couldn't even imagine it if Mackenzie or Edie or the others were hurt.

"I'll be to you in five minutes," Captain Patrick said.

"I'll be out front. Thank you, sir."

20

Damon grabbed his cheek. Blood poured between his fingers, coating his hand and running down his sleeve. "You bitch!"

Mackenzie's eyes widened. He pulled his hand away, and she saw the white of his cheekbone through the blood. The blade was far sharper than she expected, and it cut deep.

Damon put his hand over his cheek again and lunged toward Mackenzie.

She swung the blade again, catching his hand this time. He grunted as blood dripped from the tip of his index finger. Mackenzie already believed he might be indestructible, but seeing him bleeding and still moving on her made her wonder if he really was invincible.

Mackenzie backed up, her instinct telling her to flee even though she knew she had the advantage on him at the moment.

Damon's eyes tracked her movement. He moved toward her. He wasn't giving up.

Neither was she.

The chime on the doorbell signaled someone was approaching seconds before the front door slammed open.

"Hands up!" Captain Patrick shouted. His gun was trained on Damon.

"She tried to kill me. Arrest her for attempted murder," Damon spat. Blood still poured through his hand and down his wrist, but he froze where he stood.

Captain Patrick looked around the room quickly. "I see one woman bound, another injured, and my guess is the other two people here are bound and gagged, maybe knocked out. Appears to me as though it was self-defense."

Damon growled and lunged for Captain Patrick. The gun in his face made Damon stop hard.

"I wouldn't do whatever it is you're thinking about doing."

Damon put his hands up and scowled. Blood ran down his cheek.

Captain Patrick nodded and six more men swarmed into the house. Two went straight to Damon. One cuffed him while the other searched him for weapons, retrieving a gun and a knife. Another officer went straight to Edie and one went to Raina.

"You okay?" Captain Patrick asked Mackenzie.

Mackenzie nodded. "Yeah. How did you know I was here?"

Captain Patrick turned back to the door. "I brought a friend."

Holden walked in with his medical bag over his shoulder. He went straight to her. "You're okay. Are you okay? Say you're okay."

Mackenzie collapsed into his arms, the razor blade falling to the floor as she reached for him. The adrenaline that kept her fighting waned as the danger was eliminated and walked out the door.

"Oh, God, Mack. I'm so sorry. Are you hurt or just scared?"

She whimpered and pulled back. She held up her scarred hand to show where she cut it with the blade. "It's nothing compared to Edie and Raina. The FBI agents were both knocked out. I'll be fine. Help them."

"Are you sure?" Holden asked.

Mackenzie nodded. He started to walk away, but she grabbed his jacket and pulled him back for a kiss. "I love you, Holden."

He beamed at her. "I love you, too, Mack."

She smiled and stepped back. He winked at her, then went to check on the others.

Mackenzie stayed to the side and let the others work. She couldn't believe it was over. Damon was in handcuffs and going to jail. Edie was safe. Raina was safe. It was over.

DAMON SAT IN A HOLDING CELL, his cheek barely taped shut and his finger wrapped. They did the bare minimum to keep him from bleeding out. He was in pain, and he was pissed off.

And he was not going down.

He waited, biding his time. It was law for him to get a call. And he knew exactly who he was going to call.

Hours passed. More than he could keep track of. He dozed off at one point, only to jerk awake when the door to the holding cells slammed open.

"Mr. Street."

"I want my phone call," Damon demanded.

"Have you not gotten your phone call yet?" the dickhead captain asked with a smirk.

"You know I haven't. I'd like that now. Along with privacy."

"You don't get privacy," the captain snarled.

Damon grinned. "Well, I do get my call."

"Yes, you do. Hands."

Damon slid his hands through the gap in the bars and waited for the cuffs to be slapped on. Once they were, he pulled his hands back in and waited for the door to be opened. He was going to play by the rules. For now.

The captain walked him to where the phone was attached to the wall. Damon smiled and thanked the captain, waiting for him to join the other officer a few steps away before Damon lifted the receiver and dialed the number he memorized long ago.

"Yes?" the voice on the other end said.

"I'm sure you've seen the news by now."

"I have."

"I will not go down alone. I know all the secrets. More than even you know."

"Don't push it."

"You already offered me a deal."

"Which you turned down."

"And which I'm now accepting."

"You burned that bridge, Damon."

"There's only one way to burn a bridge in our business," Damon hissed.

"One minute!" the captain barked.

"Throwing my offer in the face of my representative is burning a bridge, Damon."

"And leaving me here to sing to the cops is career suicide," Damon threatened.

"I thought you had an inside man. A cop on your payroll."

"He is no longer an option."

Laughter rang through the line. "You killed the one and only person loyal to you."

"Hardly. He'd have sold me out just as quickly. He served his purpose. And now you have a choice. I can make a deal or I can get out today. Up to you, boss."

"Time's up," the captain said, approaching Damon.

Damon grinned and hung up the phone. He let the captain lead him back to the holding cell to wait.

MACKENZIE HELD Edie's hand while she waited for the doctor to release her from the hospital. Raina, Lorelei, and Adam were being treated in other rooms. Raina and Lorelei were going to be released, but Adam was being kept for a day or two for his head injury.

Holden stood in the doorway, giving them space while also standing guard.

"I can't believe you took him down. That you fought back. You were like... a total badass." Edie shook her head.

Mackenzie chuckled. "I told myself I was never going to stand by and watch someone I care about get hurt again. The night Jaclyn died, I froze. I saw Pete kill her. It happened so fast, but I was so scared that I didn't do anything. I just hid. I saved myself. And I've regretted it every day since."

"You couldn't have saved her. You know that."

Mackenzie nodded. "I know. But it still hurts to know she died."

"But you saved four people tonight."

Mackenzie sucked in a breath.

"Hell, yeah, she did," Holden said. "You should be proud of yourself."

Mackenzie nodded. She was pretty proud. It felt good to know she helped take down one of the city's worst criminals ever. To know he was going away forever, and she made it happen.

"I was terrified."

"We all were. When he knocked Adam out, I was sure he was just going to shoot all of us."

"Good or bad, that's not how he works. He wanted to draw it out. He wasn't going to let any of you live, but he was going to make sure he fed off your fear first," Mackenzie said with a shiver.

"Well, thankfully, you showed up when you did. I'm just glad it's all over. Of course, now I need to figure out where I'm going to live. I don't want to go back to the shelter, although Frannie said I could. I'm back to square one."

"Move in with me," Holden said, surprising Mackenzie and Edie.

"What?" Edie gasped, looking at the other two.

Mackenzie gawked at the man she loved and wondered why he was asking another woman to move in with him.

"Both of you," Holden clarified. "I don't like the idea of either of you being alone. My place is not huge, but it's temporary."

Mackenzie and Edie shared a look and grinned. "Sounds good," Mackenzie said. "Are you sure, though?"

Holden walked over to them and took Mackenzie's hand. "Yes. When Marcus called and said you were late for a meeting and we realized what might have happened, I felt like someone ripped my heart out and stomped on it. I don't want anything to happen to either of you."

"Thank you," Mackenzie said quietly.

"Yes, Holden, thank you," Edie said. "I hate that all of this happened, but I am really happy I met both of you."

"Me, too."

The doctor came in a short while later with Edie's paperwork, and the three of them went to Raina's room, where Lorelei was speaking to her.

"We're going to make sure you feel safe before you're on your own," Lorelei said.

"Thanks. Karli was amazing to me. She's always been such a great friend. She always spoke highly of you. You were her hero. After all this, I know why."

"Thanks," Lorelei said. "I still can't believe that piece of shit got into the house."

"Thanks to Mackenzie, we're all okay." Raina nodded to Mackenzie, Edie, and Holden, letting Lorelei know they were there.

"Are you free?" Lorelei asked.

Edie nodded. "We wanted to check on you guys. How's Adam?"

"They're going to keep him for a day or two," Lorelei said. "Where are you going to stay?"

"Holden offered to have Mackenzie and I stay with him for a while. I have no home."

"You and me both," Raina said. "Maybe we should move in together. I'm sure we'd be able to get a great apartment with our nonexistent work history and no money."

Edie laughed with Raina. They'd obviously become friends in the short time they were roommates. Edie sat on the edge of Raina's bed. "I have no doubt."

Mackenzie leaned against Holden's side and watched the other women talk. It was nice to see Edie smile. She hadn't done that much in the short time they'd known each other.

Raina was released shortly after, and they all moved to Adam's room to check on him. It wasn't long before he was falling asleep and they all filed out quietly.

"Where are you guys going now?" Mackenzie asked as they made it out the doors to the vehicles.

"Frannie has a room for me for tonight. For Lorelei, too. You guys should come. Karli, Jessica, and Stacey are going to be there, too," Raina said.

Mackenzie and Edie looked at each other, then looked at Holden.

"Up to you, ladies," Holden said.

"We'll go for a little while. I don't think I can sleep just yet anyway," Mackenzie said.

Edie nodded. "I agree."

Edie and Mackenzie talked the entire time Holden drove to Shelter in the Storm. He parked in the back, and they followed Raina and Lorelei inside.

Marcus, Francesca, Jessica, Karli, and Stacey were laughing when Mackenzie and the others walked in. They jumped up and all of them hugged each other.

"This is a good night," Francesca said. "We're so grateful to you, Mackenzie."

"I'm just happy I was in the right place at the right time." Mackenzie didn't like being the center of attention.

"Well, whatever happened, it was truly amazing. He's finally gone away, and he'll never see the light of day again. I think this calls for a celebration," Francesca said. "I'll get the champagne."

Holden and Marcus sat next to each other, talking quietly while the women passed champagne glasses around and laughed. The entire mood in the room was lighter than Mackenzie had ever seen. She smiled and laughed, enjoying time with her new friends.

"I'm so happy you're safe," Karli said, hugging Raina. "You can finally start to move on with your life now."

Raina nodded. "I'm looking forward to that. Edie and I were talking about finding an apartment. Once we have jobs and can actually pay for it."

"You are both welcome to stay here as long as you need a place," Francesca said.

"Thank you," Edie said.

"Yes, thank you," Raina said. "I just feel like I can breathe. Like I can finally start thinking about a life beyond right now."

"You can. He's going away. All the evidence against him, all the things we know he's done, he's gone. For good," Francesca said.

"Finally," Jessica said.

"Yes," Karli added.

Marcus's phone rang, and he excused himself to answer it.

Francesca poured more champagne for everyone.

Mackenzie yawned. The day was getting to her, and she was about ready to go back to Holden's and sleep. She looked at Edie and knew she was feeling the same.

"I think we might head out," Mackenzie said. "I'm getting tired. Edie?"

"Yeah, me, too," Edie said. "Thank you for inviting us over."

They all stood and hugged. They promised to be in touch and started to move toward the door when Marcus walked back into the room.

"What's wrong?" Francesca asked.

Her tone stopped Mackenzie, and the others, cold.

Marcus looked at Francesca, then Raina. His gaze stayed on Raina.

"Just say it," Raina whispered.

"Damon is free," Marcus said.

"What?" everyone gasped.

Marcus held up his phone. "I just got a call from the station. A high-powered lawyer waltzed in, got a judge to listen to him and set bail, and the lawyer paid the bail."

"He's out of jail?" Raina gasped.

"Unfortunately, he is," Marcus said.

"Oh, my God." Raina collapsed to the floor.

"This can't be real," Lorelei said.

"Unfortunately, it is. He's out. And if I had to guess, it'll be a long time before we find him again," Marcus said.

So much for a fucking celebration.

FATAL IS AVAILABLE NOW…

It was supposed to be over. Damon was arrested, and he should have gone away for good. But he's free, and Raina's in even more danger now. Adam blames himself. He let down his guard and started to fall for her. He won't let it happen again. When they go on the run, the lines are blurred. It only takes one slip to bring evil right back to their door.

BUY FATAL TODAY!

Everyone deserves justice. Even when they're no one.

Witnessing a murder was not on Frannie's bucket list.
Marcus had to find out what the curvy dancer knew.
They made a deal. She would help him, and he would find
the murderers. No one would know she was involved. She
hoped.

**Frannie and Marcus's story is available only to
subscribers.**
Sign up at https://dl.bookfunnel.com/y9ms2k2dq8 to get
FORSAKEN now.

Turn the page to read chapter one of FATAL.

FATAL

CHAPTER 1

Tears rolled down Raina London's face as she walked back into the safe house she'd called home for six weeks. Blood stained the floor, and splintered wood littered the hallway. She turned into the room that was hers and tried not to let the fear rolling through her overwhelm her. She had to be strong. She had to pack her things and get the hell out of there.

It had only been one night. One night since the man she once thought she loved broke into what was supposed to be a safe house and tried to kill her. Would have, too, if not for the heroics of the people helping Raina. She was willing to die for them, and if she thought the terror would end, she would. But she knew Damon Street. He would never give up.

Once she was dead, he'd set his sights on someone else. There was no such thing as safe if he was alive.

Lorelei Sloane, one of Raina's protectors, stood in the hallway outside the bedroom. Raina could feel the other woman's presence and was grateful for it as much as she hated it. Damon stole Raina's freedom, her sanity, her life as she knew it. And he wasn't done.

Raina stuffed the clothes she'd brought with her into a suitcase and ignored the carnage left behind. Being there again was too soon. And Damon knowing where it was meant she couldn't stay there. They were moving to another safe house. One no one would be allowed in or out of. One that would restrict Raina's already restricted world to a pinpoint.

She hated Damon. She'd never thought she could hate someone the way she hated him, but she did. If he died, she wouldn't feel an ounce of sadness. But the man was invincible. She almost wondered if he was immortal. He definitely had more than his fair share of lives.

"Are you ready?" Lorelei asked quietly.

Raina nodded, zipping up the suitcase and turning back to her one and only remaining protector. Lorelei's partner, Adam Johnson, was in the hospital. He would join them when he was out, but for the moment, it was just the two of them.

No match for Damon, if he tried again.

And he would. Raina knew he would. He hadn't stopped trying to get her back since she left him almost a year ago. After he nearly killed her. She'd never go back to him willingly. But she knew she'd never be free of him, either.

Lorelei wasn't back to full strength, but she understood Raina's need for someone she knew to be there. Adam's cousin waited in the SUV outside for them. Their driver for the day since Lorelei suffered a minor concussion. Liam was staying with Lorelei and Raina until Adam was released from the hospital. Adam's concussion was more serious, but he would be out soon.

It was a mess. A mess that could have been avoided if Raina hadn't fallen for a man who was more evil than human.

She kicked herself for the mistakes she made. For letting Damon suck her into his life. For being so weak she believed his lies when he claimed to love her and wanted to only protect her. All the therapy she had helped, until she looked into Damon's eyes again.

How did she not see him before? How did she miss the way he looked at her?

She knew the answer even as the questions rolled around in her head. She didn't want to.

Sure, he hid his true self from her for a long time. A man like him didn't show how evil he was on day one. But there were little signs. Moments, snippets, clues. Raina ignored them. She thought she was crazy for thinking Damon was anything less than the perfect man he presented himself as.

And people died because of her error in judgement.

Raina followed Lorelei out to the waiting SUV and sat in the backseat. She struggled to breathe or think or function. Her mind was numb, like the rest of her.

Damon is free.

Marcus's words from the night before rattled around in her mind. After months of hunting him, he was out within hours. All the hell he put her through, the people he killed, the lives he ruined, all wiped clean by one lawyer in an expensive suit.

Raina was going to be sick.

Liam slowed and turned into the driveway of a small

house. The garage door opened in front of them, and he rolled the SUV right into the garage. He turned off the vehicle, and they all waited until the garage doors slid closed behind them.

"Home sweet home," Liam said.

Raina reached for a smile, but it was hard to find one. Liam seemed nice enough, friendly and kind and smart as hell, but he wasn't Adam. She'd gotten used to Adam and Lorelei. The three of them got along easily. She fit with them. But Liam...

Raina just wanted it all to be over. Liam was fine. Lorelei was fine. Adam was fine. Raina just wanted to go home. Sleep in a bed she picked out. Take an endless hot shower and forget all about Damon Street.

Too bad that wasn't going to happen anytime soon.

Adam Johnson closed his eyes and groaned. He hated being stuck in the hospital. He knew it was where he needed to be, but he still hated it.

When Raina walked in that morning with Lorelei, and they told Adam that Damon Street was free, Adam shook with rage. He started yanking off the pads stuck to his body. He was not going to leave his partner and their witness alone. He couldn't. He had to be there to help them.

Of course, Lorelei and Raina both forced him back into bed, and a nurse came in and reattached all the leads, annoying Adam to no end. He'd never been a fan of hospitals, and knowing he was leaving two women who meant a lot to him without additional protection infuriated him.

Street surprised Adam when he broke into the safe house and knocked Adam out before he had a chance to warn the others. He later learned Street also got to Lorelei. Raina and Edie were vulnerable, and Street would have killed all four of them if Mackenzie hadn't shown up when she did.

Adam's stomach rolled at the thought.

He knew the important thing was that they were all alive. But he still felt like a failure to have gone down first. He didn't even put up a fight and slow the bastard down. Street surprised Adam and cold-cocked him as soon as Adam saw him.

Failure was common. It was expected. It was something all agents experienced. He'd lost witnesses before. Lost coworkers. Lost leads. But none of them were as important to him as Raina.

Not that he was willing to admit to anyone else that he'd developed feelings for her. That was between Adam and the shower wall.

His phone buzzed with a text alert. Adam snatched his phone from the table next to his bed and swiped to open Liam's text.

All set. Moved in. No one will get close.

Adam let go of a breath he hadn't been aware he was holding. He knew Liam would protect Lorelei and Raina, but it still grated on Adam that he wasn't there to do it himself.

Thanks. Hopefully I'm free tomorrow and can relieve you.

No worries. Caitlyn's staying with Taylor and Dex. We're all used to this. Rest and recover so you're 100.

Adam set the phone on the table again and tried to focus his mind. The goal hadn't changed. Take down Damon Street. The problem now was that the man was free and knew who they all were. They had to not only find him again, but make sure the arrest warrant meant a judge wouldn't grant bail. At any level.

Adam thought they'd done that, but they were all wrong. And Street was out.

A nurse came in a little later and asked Adam how he was doing. The guy was a sports fan and liked to talk, so Adam passed the time hearing stories from him about local teams. It meant Adam didn't feel so completely abandoned and alone.

Fucking hospital.

The nurse left, and Adam stared at the walls again. He thought living in a safe house was boring. He would never complain again. About a safe house, a stakeout, anything.

Afternoon turned to night, and Adam fell asleep. His dreams were a jumbled mess of Street, Raina being hurt, and purple fucking pansies. That last one Adam couldn't explain. Weird shit happened in his mind.

Morning came again, and the doctor finally said Adam could leave the hospital. It was the best damn news ever.

He let Liam know, and Liam arranged transportation to take Adam to the new safe house.

Only another hour or so and he'd be back with Raina and Lorelei.

"Are we being followed?" Adam asked Dunn, Liam's boss. They'd met once before, but Adam didn't know Dunn well.

"No," Dunn answered. He checked all his mirrors again. "I've been changing direction and going in weird routes to watch. I haven't seen anyone following us."

"We can't risk exposing the safe house again."

"I know," Dunn growled.

Adam didn't know why Dunn was annoyed by that. It wasn't like Dunn was the one who was knocked out with a gun to the back of his head.

"We have security on this place twenty-four-seven. No one will get anywhere close without us knowing."

"What kind of security?"

"Motion and heat, signal blockers, and personal surveillance."

"You're going to have someone watching us?"

"Yes," Dunn said. "Outside the house, at least. We have the ability to add cameras inside, but we haven't done that yet. Is that something you want?"

Adam shook his head and winced. His brain was still scrambled, and sudden movements made him nauseous. "No, outside should be fine. Especially in this cold. You'll be able to pick up on heat signatures."

"Yep." Dunn turned into a driveway and pulled straight into a garage, parking beside an identical SUV. He closed the garage door, then got out.

Adam followed Dunn inside, wanting to see with his own eyes that Lorelei and Raina were okay. And Liam. He should worry about his cousin, too, but Liam hadn't been attacked.

Liam met them at the garage door, his hand on the weapon in his holster. He looked at them both, then past them to make sure there wasn't a third person sending them in at gunpoint. Liam relaxed and nodded to his boss, then hugged Adam gently.

"Glad you're alive."

"Same," Adam said. "How're Lorelei and Raina?"

"Resting. It's been a long few days," Liam said.

"Yeah, it has. How's this place?"

Liam shrugged, but Adam knew his cousin outfitted the house with every toy he could find. It was an F-BOMB safe house, one they were borrowing since the FBI safe house was clearly not as safe as they'd all expected.

"Windows and doors are tagged. Including the egress. Cameras at all the entrances. Heat and motion around the whole perimeter. No one will get within a mile of this place without us knowing."

"What if they pull into the driveway and just start shooting?"

"Windows and walls are all bulletproof. Won't stop them forever, but should slow down whoever shows up long enough for you to get out."

"And how would we do that?"

"Secondary exit out the back. Garage opens both ways so you can drive out the back and disappear into the woods, then get back on the road half-a-mile south of here."

"Jesus, you really thought of everything."

"Not our first rodeo," Dunn said with meaning. They lost someone. No more chances. Adam respected that.

"What do I need to know?" Adam asked the other two.

Dunn and Liam exchanged a glance.

"Tell me."

"Street's in the wind. As expected. The lawyer who bailed him out is not talking. Says his client will appear in court if there are charges that are substantiated. He's calling foul on everything. The way evidence was collected, the circumstantial nature of it all, everything. He's saying Street isn't guilty and that he's been framed for everything we have him on."

"What about beating the shit out of his girlfriend? Doesn't that count for anything around here?" Adam barked. He'd seen the police report from the night Raina left Street. The bruises on her face and body. The X-rays showing the broken bones. The fear in her eyes. If nothing else, they should have been able to hold him for that.

"He has a court date. But the rest? We know it's all him, but our proof isn't good enough." Liam's voice was soothing but did nothing to calm Adam's frustration.

"Are you fucking kidding me? He knocked me out cold, same with Lorelei. Doesn't that count for anything? We're FBI agents. Attacking us and holding Raina and Edie at gunpoint should be something worth holding the fucker on." Adam was baffled. What the hell kind of lawyer wanted a man like Damon Street out in the world? The only answer was a crooked one.

"The judge agreed with the lawyer," Dunn told Adam. "We believe they're both involved in Street's organization."

"Fucking hell. Makes sense, though. So, now what?"

"We play their game and we nail him. We can't stop now when we're this close," Dunn said.

"I agree. It sounds like we need to take out the judge and the lawyer, too, though. Otherwise, Street will keep going free."

Dunn and Liam nodded.

The three men talked a little longer, then Liam and Dunn left. Adam insisted he was okay and could handle things, but once they left, he sat on the couch with his eyes closed, willing the throbbing in his brain to subside.

Ten minutes later, the squeak of a door down the hall had Adam lifting his head and pretending to be fine again.

Raina stepped out of the room and looked both directions. When she saw him on the couch, her lips lifted in a ghost of a smile. "Hey."

"Hey." Adam was striving for casual, but seeing her made his entire body ache. He wanted to wrap her in his arms and protect her from all the evil in the world. He wanted to kiss her senseless and make sure she never knew hate again. He wanted to erase the bruises and scrapes from her body and keep any harm from ever coming to her again.

But he couldn't do any of that. Because he was her protector, not her boyfriend. She was recovering from an abusive asshole of an ex, and the last thing she needed was an overprotective asshole trying to convince her to be his woman.

Nope. He had to keep his feelings to himself and treat her like any other witness.

"How are you feeling?" he asked when she got closer.

Raina sat next to him on the couch and tucked her feet under her. She shrugged. She propped her elbow on the back of the couch and put her head in her hand, then cringed and changed positions.

Street dragged her around by her hair. She was lucky he didn't rip chunks out from what Lorelei told Adam. One more thing Adam wanted the sick piece-of-shit to pay for.

"I'm tired," Raina finally said. "I feel like I could sleep for a week, but when I close my eyes, I see him." Her words went soft at the end. She drew in a breath. "I never should have left him."

"Why would you say that?"

"He would have killed me by now if I'd stayed there. Then all the people I care about wouldn't be in danger, and I wouldn't be living in fear. I know he's going to kill me. He's not going to stop until he does. All I'm doing right now is delaying the inevitable. And the fear is getting to me. He's thriving on it, feeding on it. He knows I'm scared, and he's enjoying playing with me. With all of us. And I hate it."

"I know. But we'll get him. We'll take him down, and he'll never hurt you again."

Raina breathed a mirthless laugh. "I thought that before. I don't think I can believe that. Not now. Not after the last few days. The only way Damon will ever stop is if he's dead."

Adam saw the determination in her gaze. She knew Street better than anyone else. She was right. Adam knew in his soul she was.

Which meant there was only one answer. Damon Street had to die.

READ **FATAL** TODAY

ABOUT THE AUTHOR

USA TODAY Bestselling Author Mary E Thompson spent most of her childhood wishing she had a few less curves. She hid in the pages of books because her favorite characters never cared what size her clothes were. Now, neither does Mary, and she writes stories that celebrate women like her. Real women who have curves, chase dreams, and find love, because we should all be happy, no matter our dress size.

Mary spends her non-writing time with her husband and two kids, watching too much TV, cheering for her hometown football team (Go Bills!), and hiding chocolate from her family.

Visit https://MaryEThompson.com/ to sign up for Mary's newsletter, **Romancing the Curves**. Subscribers get free ebooks and other fun stuff, like exclusive, members only content and giveaways, plus are the first to know about new releases and sales!